L. Weiss

Talmudic and Other Legends

Second Edition

L. Weiss

Talmudic and Other Legends
Second Edition

ISBN/EAN: 9783337163471

Printed in Europe, USA, Canada, Australia, Japan

Cover: Foto ©Andreas Hilbeck / pixelio.de

More available books at **www.hansebooks.com**

TALMUDIC AND OTHER LEGENDS

FACTS AND FICTIONS FROM OLDEN TIMES.

REVISED AND ENLARGED.

TRANSLATED AND COMPILED BY

L. WEISS.

SECOND EDITION.

NEW YORK:
PRESS OF STETTINER, LAMBERT & CO.,
22, 24 & 26 READE STREET.
1888.

PREFACE TO FIRST EDITION.

In entering upon the task of translating and compiling legends, it is meet to have a proper understanding of the adaptability of legends.

Legends are narratives conceived by fancy and imagination, but they often impart valuable lessons, illustrative and descriptive, in their allegoric manner. Pulpit speakers not unfrequently employ them to good advantage in elucidating sublime precepts and divine doctrines. A legend, notwithstanding its mythical and imaginary character, conveys sometimes ideas expressive of truth incarnate and thought sublime.

The Talmud abounds in legends, but I have taken special care to compile only such as shall be instructive as well as entertaining to the reader of whatever denomination.

In the " Facts, " I have chronicled many historical events which the reader will not fail to notice.

In the " Fictions," the imaginative talents of our ancient rabbins and sages are so depicted that our esteem, reverence, and respect for them can be but heightened.

In the " Translations " I have added or omitted as the occasion required, either to substitute some idiom unemployable in the English language, or to avoid superfluities unnecessary in the version ;

but I have, in every instance, taken care not to destroy the property and originality.

As to the superscriptions, I have adapted them to the lessons the subject is to convey. Thus I send out this little work into the world, not as my original production, but as a little flower garden containing some rare plants, collected from vast gardens cultivated by gardeners far superior in talent and learning to the humble compiler—the rabbis of olden times.

I may not have suited the tastes of all, nor is that my expectation, for

> " He that writes,
> Or makes a feast, more certainly invites
> His judges than his friends; there's not a guest
> But will find something wanting, or ill-drest,"

but fondly hope that this little volume will find favor with many, and they will aid me in scattering, to some extent, the grains of liberality and profundity of our sages of yore, thus causing the slanderers of the Talmud and ancient Hebrew literature to blush. With this object in view, I commend it to the kind indulgence of the reader.

L. WEISS.

HELENA, ARK., June, 1884, 5644 A.M.

PREFACE TO SECOND EDITION.

Encouraged by the financial success of my first edition, and the favorable criticism it has received from the press, both religious and secular, notwithstanding its many defects, owing to the utter lack of experience of the publishers in book printing—having been published at Helena, Ark., a village—I issue a second edition, amended, revised, and enlarged, making it more interesting and instructive, as well as compatible with all readers of whatever denomination, and hope that it will receive the same welcome as its predecessor received.

L. WEISS.

COLUMBUS, GA., June, 1888, 5648 A.M.

CONTENTS.

CONTENTS.   ix

ORIGIN OF SHAKESPEARE'S SHYLOCK.

It was on a bright October night after the gates of the Ghetto* were closed that a darkly clad gentleman, apparently of high rank, tall and stately in form and commanding in appearance, stood outside as if anxiously waiting for some one to come. Presently the gate was opened and a small individual, seemingly of low rank, came out, and the following dialogue ensued, opened by the first gentleman:

"Well, Portica, what have you accomplished? Have you succeeded in gaining me the inclination of the prudish Jewess? Have you moved heaven and hell to gratify my desire?"

"I have accomplished nothing," answered the little man, whose voice was that of a woman. "I have accomplished nothing. The maiden remains as prudish as ever, insusceptible to flattery and threats alike. I might have shown her heaven it-

---

* Quarters assigned for the habitation of Jews, originally at Rome and afterwards in other cities. These quarters were inclosed by walls and the gates leading to the principal part of the city were closed at sundown, and no Jew was allowed to pass them after this hour A guard stood there for this purpose, and only by special permission was he allowed to open the gate for Jews.

self and offered her all it contains, and she would still remain invincible and insuperable. Grief-stricken as she is, with tearful eyes and ghastly countenance she threw herself at my feet, clasping my knees convulsively, and under lamentable sobs begged for mercy and compassion for her despairing and unfortunate father. Indeed, that Jewish maiden unnerved me so that I had to struggle hard to conquer my emotions and remain firm, repeating the price of your mercy. I, Signor Zavello, have done my part faithfully. I have used all exertions, leaving nothing that I could do undone. I have praised your youth, your beauty, and your prominence, and described your wealth, your love, and your affection for her; then I have portrayed in agonizing terms the doom that awaited Shylock, her father, for not being able to meet the payment of the thousand sequins* he owes you, but in response she only found words of begging and imploring for mercy. She entreated, she whined, she wrung her hands—she drew from her finger a diamond ring, a relic and inheritance of her mother, offering it to me. Her festal attire she placed at my disposal that I should plead in her behalf, but I remained immovable.

"When she saw that all was of no avail, she sprang to her feet like an exasperated lioness, her countenance assuming an appearance of determination, and with utter indignation she exclaimed, 'So my father *must* die!—*let him die!* My igno-

---

* A sequin is about three English shillings.

miny and disgrace *shall not* and *will not* be his ransom! Nor does my father desire it. Ah, let him die, I will soon follow him and my beloved mother—and you—' addressing herself to me— 'you bestial pandress, leave my sight or else I will lay hands on you!' So infuriated was she that her two black eyes sparkled like burning coal, her dark disheveled hair waved, like they were snakes, around her ivory neck, and her cheeks were burning red from fury. I deemed it the safest and wisest to leave the apartment, and I hurried away."

"And shall I abandon this precious prize!" exclaimed Zavello. "Shall I be unable to possess that pretty Jewess! Shall I renounce the charming Jessica! No, I will not!" "Well," said Portica, "I would not go again in that Jewish house. I would not venture again to approach that Jewish maiden, and I would advise you too, Antonio, to be careful and precautious."

"Precautious!" interrupted him Zavello with a forced and satiric laugh. "These Hebrew *vermin* only bend when you tread on them. Nay, if everything has hitherto failed—if no means could bring the stubborn and stiffnecked Jewess to subjection —in one thing I shall surely succeed. To-morrow I will cause to glorify the October Festival* of the Romans in such spectacular manner that even in

---

* October was with the Romans a month of festivals. The eleventh was the Meditrinalia, in honor of Meditrina, on the thirteenth was Faunalia, on the fifteenth the Enquiria, and thus the first of the month was ushered in with a chief of festivals.

Diocletian's time, when the defenceless Christians were cast before the wild beasts, such was not seen. Preparatory to this I have to-day spent gifts in profusion among the populace, and donations in abundance among the poor. This will undoubtedly make it appear that I am grateful for the favorable decision that was rendered in my suit against the Jew whom I sued for the thousand sequins. To-morrow the whole city will be in locomotion ! Ah, what noise and turbulence there will be ! The laziest sleeper will rise early. As for our Holy Father, I will but pay him the debt which we all owe him in his own coin. He thinks that with his justice and strictness he can suppress everything and trample under his feet our old prerogatives. He will now experience how we can utilize his strict justice, and how the Baron can turn his own weapon against him." A satiric laugh then rang into the air which concluded the audience and, with a few formal salutatories, the two parted and were soon lost sight of in the darkness of the night.

.   .   .   .

Felix Peretti, Cardinal De Montralto, was at this time pope, known as Sixtus V. He has given glorious examples of true Christianity, and above all has established strict justice. During five years of his popedom, Rome was raised to the highest standard of law and order, and the church was governed by righteousness and justness instead of anarchy as theretofore. The barons and nobleman who ruled and ruined the state he had

shorn of their licentious sovereignty, so, that wherever the arm of Sixtus reached security and justice
prevailed. To ferret out all evil he would often
leave at evenings and nights the Vatican, garbed in
various robes, and visit some dense quarters in
order to acquaint himself with the necessities to
restore law and order. To this effect he had a
secret passage to the Vatican and nobody knew of
his plans. The night our history speaks of, Sixtus
was robed as a beggar and was rambling in various
directions; when in front of the Ghetto he saw the
tall gentleman full of anxiety and expectancy. He
knew that something must have been up, and he
withdrew into a remote place where he could not
be seen, but he could overhear all the above conversation. It was the very gifts and presents dis-
tributed by Antonio Zavello that brought out the
pope that day, for he knew that without benefit
to himself in some way or other that baron was
not so generous. He went out as a beggar, and
received alms like all beggars, and chatted with
them like an equal. In this capacity he conversed
with an old mendicant, experienced in the profes-
sion, and he elicited this statement: " Antonio Zavello's desire will be gratified to-morrow, wherefore
he indulges in this almsgiving to-day. I pity the
poor Jew whom he loaned the money. He was a
fool to pledge a pound of flesh—now he will feel
it, and the people will have the grandest spectacle
they ever witnessed." The pope was surprised to
hear this and went into detailed inquiries and
learned that this infamous verdict was the decision

of the court. His heart yearned for justice, and
he hurried to the Ghetto to learn all the particu-
lars of the case. He spent the day in this way,
and it was drawing towards evening when he left
the Ghetto. He saw a Jewish maiden hurrying
into her quarters, she looked the picture of despair and her features resembled almost that of a
maniac. The pope, placing himself right before
her path, asking the reason of her excitement and
why she so hurried, but she begged to be excused,
giving as the reason of her haste the lateness of the
hour and the fear of being locked out from the
Ghetto. The pope reached a coin to the gate-
guard, whereby he assured her that the gate would
be opened to her even after closing time, but she
still looked distrustful and begged to be let alone.
The sweet demeanor of Sixtus, however, quoting
to her words of divine origin such as, " Behold
the Keeper of Israel shall neither sleep nor slumber (Psalm ci. 4) seemed to inspire her with
more confidence, and she listened to the soothing
words of the great prelate in humble garb. He
was telling her how the mighty Goliath was conquered by the lad David, and how the exiled boy
Joseph, by his advice, saved thousands from starvation, " is it then not possible, my child," asked
he, " that I may be able to advise or help you in
your trouble?" She then broke her reticence and
told the sweet comforter that she just came from
Zavello; that her name was Jessica, the daughter
of Shylock, a Jew, who foolishly signed a pledge
of a pound of flesh from the nearest spot to his

heart, in case he should not be able to pay a debt of a thousand sequins, and, "alas! alas!"—here she burst into tears—"Zavello intends to carry into effect to-morrow the conditions thus made." "Why," asked Sixtus, "was your father so careless in signing a document like that, when the Jews otherwise are shrewd and foresighted?" "Ah!" explained Jessica, "Zavello appeared to be our friend, visiting our house for the past year almost daily, and my father owing him for rent, and some cash advancement which became due, he was perplexed and agitated. He asked for further time, but Zavello was reluctant in granting this without security, which my father was unable to furnish, and Zavello proposed, which seemed to be more a joke than earnestness, that he would accept as security a pound of flesh of the nearest spot to my father's heart, and, he, taking it for a joke, appended his name to this contract"—here she sobbed bitterly, as she concluded, "and now the *human tiger* wants to relinquish his claim only at the expense of my ignominy, to which neither I would consent nor would my father desire it." The kind pope whispered more words of hope and comfort into her ears and bid her a pleasant good-night. She hastily entered the gate and he remained there in deep pondering. This was the time when he overheard the conversation of Antonio Zavello and his pander.

. . . .

Early next morning the place called Bocca Della Verita was the scene of gathering of spectators to the coming event. The throng was so great that some could find no standing room and they crowded up on windows and roofs near by. This was the place where Shylock was brought to by guards of armed soldiers, his coreligionists standing in awe and despair afar off, with only two at his side supporting him, which made it appear so much more heart-rending.

The doomed Jew was weeping bitterly and praying—praying so loud that his voice and words were heard audibly, but it aroused no sympathy, and he was just concluding his prayer, in the words all prayers of Israelites end, "In Thy hand, O God, I commend my spirit!" when the great silence of spectators was broken by murmurs perceptible in the crowd. All eyes turned toward the side whence the murmur issued, and behold, a rider, apparently a senator of the Holy See, pressing his way to the place of execution, arriving not too soon to give a commanding "Halt!" to the officer who was about in the act of applying the knife to Shylock's flesh.

Thus stopping further proceedings, he stepped before the cruel baron, addressing him in a cordial manner: "Antonio Zavello, his holiness, our father, requests you through me, his senator, to withdraw your strict measures which you are about to carry out on the poor Hebrew."

"I simply demand my right," replied Zavello somewhat supremely, "and his holiness will assuredly not be inclined to deprive me of this."

"Most assuredly not," asserted the senator significantly. "But a crime the Hebrew has not committed, and the thousand sequins he owes you I have with me to refund your claim ; accept them, then, and let mercy precede right."

"The pledge is forfeited," declared Zavello, and I care not for the money. I want the flesh of the Jew." The senator became stern, and in words that conveyed importance, he once more addressed the baron : " Antonio Zavello, I call upon you, in the name of his holiness, for the third time to relinquish your claim on the Hebrew, Shylock, who is known as an honest and an upright man, since the money he owes you is forthcoming ; " to which Zavello replied disdainfully : " My determination is unchangeable. I insist upon my right!" " Well, then," said the senator addressing himself to the officials and executives, " if such is the case, we will admit a witness who has incontrovertible evidence in favor of the Hebrew," and at a signal the pope's military, headed by himself, sprang into sight as if by magic, and in another moment Antonio stood face to face with the just pope who, in a thundering voice, addressed him :

" Antonio Zavello ! I am that witness, and I bear testimony to your villainy. I overheard your conversation last night with one Portico, which is evidence that you hypocritically show yourself a good Christian, while, in fact, you are a traitor to, and the ruin of, Christianity. You claim that your demand and proceeding is your right, and it is justice ; bear then in mind that there is also a law existing which prohibits, under penalty of death,

any relationship whatsoever of a Christian with a
Jewess, of which you are guilty, and to which I
bear testimony. I then give you one hour to pray
and prepare to die for this offence, and the Hebrew
shall receive the thousand sequins I had ready for
you, as indemnity for the pang and suffering you
prepared for him." Then turning to the Israelites
that stood by, he gave orders to take Shylock to
his daughter and friends.

This romance of Italian fiction undoubtedly
must have given Shakespeare material to write his
" Merchant of Venice." Knowing, however, that
the people were immature and disinclined to receive a drama which should favor the Jew, he
reversed the denominal characters and made some
other changes conforming to his ideas, never thinking probably that an imaginative fiction should so
infest the heart with prejudice for a race as did the
romance of the Merchant of Venice.

BEWARE OF HYPOCRITES.

Once upon a time, long, long ago, there lived in a city in the Orient a man of profound knowledge and unlimited learning.

> He was wise as he was old,
> Truth his words to all unroll'd.

He had but one child, a son, who was very much attached to his aged father who, at this time, lay prostrated by lingering illness. The devout son was sitting at the bedside of his father, weeping silently over the supposed approach of his last moments, who seemed to have fallen into a slight relieving slumber. But it was only for a short duration, for he soon awoke and mustered all the strength he could to erect himself into a sitting posture. He beckoned his beloved Samai to his bedside, and in feeble voice began his last admonition:

"My son! oh, my son!" said he, "I f—e—e—l m—y e—n—d i—s dr—aw—ing n—i—gh! ac- c—e—pt m—y l—l—a—s—st w—o—r—d—s—— th—e—r—e i—s"——he pointed to a little chest in a corner of the humble abode, hardly able to utter any more words distinctly, his eyes resting fixed at the corner, and his hand and figure still pointing to the chest; he wanted to force out some words yet, and hardly audible said: "Be—be—

w—w—a—re o—f—f—f hy—th—e—r—re the—r"
He could not finish the sentence.   He sank back
and expired.

> " Before decay's effacing fingers,
> Have swept the lines where beauty lingers."

The funeral and proper time allotted to mourning was over before Samai had for the first
time thought of the chest, and opening it found
nothing more than a sealed letter containing some
useful hints for the guidance of his youthful life ;
and the concluding words written in large letters
with three underlines, "BEWARE OF HYPO-
CRITES!" which he understood must have been
the words his father wanted to utter ere he died.

Samai inherited all the virtues and qualities of
his father, and carried his name untarnished from
boyhood to manhood.   He lived in lonely blessed-
ness,

> " But after time he deemed to see,
> It is not good alone to be,"

and concluded to lead to the hymeneal altar one
of the most fair damsels, whom he chose, not for
her wealth or riches, but for her qualities of virtue
and modesty.   To God he raised his voice in
prayer of praise and thanksgiving that he had
found such precious jewel, for " a virtuous wife
is the crown of her husband " (Prov. xii. 4) said
Solomon the wise, and

> Samai with his pious wife
> Led a happy, blissful life.

Once so it happened that there was a grand fair
of beautiful and extraordinary exhibitions of the

rarest wares, and the affectionate husband urged his beloved wife to dress and attend with him the fair that they might see the exposition, and she might choose something for herself, which he was willing to make her a present of; but she protested seriously. "Were it not a gross violation of a woman's chaste qualities? Samai, my dear," said she, "you are guileless and may not be aware how wicked men are, and how easily they are tempted by dress and appearance. May I not be the cause of some men conceiving evil inclinations, when I thus should appear in public? No, no! I will not go—you better go alone.

> A pious wife, a virtuous spouse,
> Is best protected in the house."

Awestruck stood the husband, intently listening to his wife's declaration, and his father's last warning and will forced itself into his memory, reverberating in his mind, "*Beware of hypocrites !*" O God, could it be that the love of his admiration, the affection of his soul was a hypocrite? His heart felt like bursting, and he silently withdrew, visiting the exposition alone, not for the sake of seeing the rarities, but for the sake of drowning his suspicious pang amidst the throng and merriment; but the wound so suddenly inflicted penetrated too deep to heal so quickly. His feelings, in thinking that his pious and talented wife considered him an insufficient protector in public, were so hurt that happiness almost forsook his breast, and yet, after maturer consideration, he thought, might this not

be real purity? Might not his Miriam have
spoken out of sheer innocence? In justice to her,
therefore, and in order to restore that felicity so
suddenly vanished, he concluded to test this, for
which purpose he contrived a plan. The following day he announced to his beloved wife that urgent business called him away from home, and that
he would have to leave her for a few days. Miriam
was shocked at this announcement. She felt
miserable at the thought of being left alone, but as
it was inevitable, she fell on her husband's neck
weeping and kissing him with most tender affec-
tions, and Samai nearly disbanded all his suspi-
cions, yet he was bent on the trial. The words of
his father, "*Beware of hypocrites*," recurred to his
mind, though he loved Miriam as only man can
love. He believed her an angel,

> "Yet he was jealous, though he did not show it,
> For jealousy dislikes the world to know it."

His horse was saddled and ready, he kissed away
the tears of his adored wife, and bidding her a
tender adieu he lifted himself in the saddle and
away he rode. Not very far did he travel, however, before he drew the reigns of the horse to
return whence he started, and by the time it was
dark, Samai was in the city again taking up his
quarters at an inn. He tarried there a while, then
leaving his horse, he wended his way towards his
own residence. It was near midnight, silence prevailed all around when he stood before his house.
His breast was filled with presentiments when he

discovered the outer door unfastened and unse-
cured. His heart throbbed and his courage
almost failed him at the idea to steal on his
wife unawares. He felt as if he would commit an
unpardonable wrong, but his happiness depended
on this, his jealousy could only be erased by this
action, and he entered boldly, ascending the stairs
till he reached the door of his wife's apartment,
which he quickly opened without notice and
warning, and, oh horror!—his suspicion was realized! and furthermore, would he not have beat a
hasty retreat, his wife's paramour would have
felled him by a dagger.

> "Oh! colder than the wind that freezes
>   Founts, that but now in sunshine play'd,
> To that congealing pang, that seizes
>   That trusting bosom when betray'd."

How dark and dreary was the night! Not a star
was visible on the celestial expanse! And amid the
stillness of the slumbering city there was but one
pedestrian in the streets, to whom all was doubly
dark, and that was Samai. Fearing to tarry in his
own house that night, he was wandering the
streets when some officers of the law seized him,
and took him to the prison where he was cast into
a cell, there to await his doom, what for he knew
not. Fain would he have given his life, though
guiltless of any offense, if his name would only remain untarnished, were his thoughts while he lan-
guished in prison.

Next day he was taken before the Kalif (judge),
where he learned that the Sultan's treasury was

robbed, and by advice of a dervish (an Islam priest), the streets were searched, and Samai being the only pedestrian at such late hour, he was arrested and imprisoned. Alas, alas! he could not even prove his innocence! All assertions were of no avail, and according to existing laws he was sentenced to be beheaded.

> " How sweetly could I lay my head
>   Within the cold grave's silent breast,
>   When sorrow's tears no more are shed,—
>   No more the ills of life molest ! "

might poor Samai have thought, but to die as a criminal is bitter! And yet there seemed no salvation for him. A meek dervish came to him in the prison, and in the sweetest words imaginable urged him to confess and repent, begging him to accept Mohammed's faith. His exceeding display of piety caused Samai to ask himself, " Is he not a HYPOCRITE? " This dervish visited him over and over again, employing himself with seeming anxiety with the welfare of the soul and future bliss of the poor prisoner, which he asserted could only be had if he confessed, which Samai could never and would never do, innocent as he was. · The time arrived, and he was led to the scaffold, preceded by an escort of soldiers, headed by the executioner and the pious dervish. Arrived at a place where a heap of dung lay piled, the dervish bid the procession to carefully pass around the spot, " for," said he, " we might tread on and kill some of the worms, and it were sinful to thus destroy God's creatures."

"A creature of amphibious nature,
On land a beast, a fish in water;
That always preys on grace or sin,
A sheep without, a wolf within."

This piece of hypocrisy Samai could endure no longer. Was he not God's creature, and yet was not spared, while this meek dervish might have been able to assist him in procuring evidence establishing his guiltlessness if he was so humane and so divine? Yet he pities the worms, and can see a human being led to the scaffold. And he called for the principal official, to whom he declared that *it was the dervish who robbed the Sultan's treasury*. The procession was caused to halt, and the dervish was apprised of this information, which, for the moment, and coming so unawares, visibly filled him with consternation. This brought among the officials a hurried consultation, and this delay so enraged the heretofore meek dervish that, in his forgetfulness, sprang with his horse on the innocent worms, killing thousands of them himself. He attempted to inspire the officials with patriotism in carrying out the mandate of the law, and he called upon them in the name of the country, Mohammed and God not to falter; but this delay reached the ear of the Kalif, who being a just judge, quickly dispatched a horseman after the procession, and they were ordered to return. The dervish seeing his plan thwarted, sought opportunity to abscond, but he was taken into custody and placed into the hands of the authorities. A search at his residence really revealed a part of the stolen treasures, and Samai was released. The Kalif, astonished at Samai's conduct, asked him how he knew that the dervish was the thief, and why he did not disclose it sooner, instead of risking his life. To which Samai first related his father's last will, then explained that he knew not of the guilt of the dervish. " But," said he, " seeing the great hypocrisy he displayed, and becoming aware that he was the court dervish, who generally has free access to the Sultan's palace, I risked the accusation. I had nothing more to lose, my life was mine no longer, and I could only regain it, or lose it any way, consequently I have denounced him." Meanwhile the officials were actively in search of the robbed treasures yet unfound, and they have discovered them at the house of a lady the dervish often visited, and were brought before the Kalif, together with the woman.

At her entrance, she perceived Samai at the side of the Kalif, and she shrieked, and fainted away. Samai sprang to his feet, his countenance became ghastly, his whole form shook like a leaf, and his lips were clasped as in agonizing pain. This the Kalif could not fail to see, and, seeming strange to him, asked for an explanation. Samai's manly figure was bent, and, the tears coursing down his cheeks, he began. " O Miriam, Miriam! It is my wife, Miriam! She accused of complicity of this crime!" And the whole of the matter became disclosed.

That memorable night when the treasury of the Sultan was robbed, the dervish, who was the robber, took a part of it immediately to Miriam, and was in her company just at the time when her husband unexpectedly returned, as related. The dervish grasped a dagger, and would have ended Samai's life would he not have fled. What was now best to do for the dervish—he quickly decided to go to the Kalif, and advised to search the streets and arrest all out so late at night, knowing that Samai must have been out. The plot was a shrewd one and a successful one. The Kalif saw it all clear, and ordered the execution of the dervish, but, in behalf of Miriam, Samai prostrated himself, pleading and supplicating for mercy, which, at length, was granted, and she was released. But they have not lived together thereafter, although he still loved her, which was evident from the fact how piteously he implored the Kalif in her behalf. He secured her pardon, and provided for her sufficiently to last her for lifetime ; but his happiness was marred, his bliss destroyed, and the wound was incurable. He lived a solitary life of piety and purity, with the counsel of his dying father deeply engraven in his memory and heart: " BEWARE OF HYPOCRITES ! "

—*Kav Hajashar*, 52.

THE HELP OF GOD.

Over two centuries ago, there lived in the city of Prague a poor Jew, Rabbi Pinchas, who was a pious and an upright man. His humble occupation was that of a buyer and seller of junks and all second-hand articles, in daytime, and occupying many hours of the night with the study of Jewish law and lore.

With all his energy and hard work, R. Pinchas was unable to earn a sufficiency to support his household, and would often have suffered want and privation were it not that a kind count took a fancy to him and extended him many a help.

Every Friday Pinchas would come to the count, and the nobleman would ask him what he earned that week and what it lacked to keep him during his Sabbath and further, which he would liberally add. Pinchas was undoubtedly very grateful for this generosity, but his pious zeal prompted him to recognize in the count an angel of God and, instead of expressing personal thanks, he would always say: "Thank God! who forsaketh not His children, he hath helped me again," or something to this effect. Often the count would ask after some holiday, to which he helped Pinchas liberally, how he passed them, and Pinchas would answer: "God hath helped." Once the count ill-took his demeanor and, thinking him an ungrateful man, he muttered to himself, " I heap upon this Jew kindness upon kindness, helping him to be able to keep his Sabbath and his holidays, and yet he thanks his God that He had helped him. I will once see how his God will help him if I shall withhold my charity from him, especially now that the Passover is coming on.

The time approached, and Pinchas as usual came to see his benefactor and humbly informed him that next day would be Passover eve. But how shocked was poor Pinchas when the count told him : " Dear Pinchas, I am now somewhat embarrassed financially, and am very sorry that I cannot help you as I always did ; you must try to get your *matzos* (unleavened bread) the best way you can. I hope the God of Israel will help you in some other way ; " Pinchas only shrugged his shoulders and sorrowfully said : " Well, what is to be done? God will help," and gave the count a friendly salute and departed for home. We can imagine the sad disappointment of the poor wife and the ragged little children when he apprised them of the unpleasant news that the count gave him nothing. Every holiday that nobleman would send clothing for the little ones and other necessities, and just now when he had a very bad week and scarcely bread in the house, poor Pinchas for the first time had to leave him without receiving the least aid. His wife was ill-humored about it, but not a murmur escaped her lips ; and he, like nothing would be the matter, retired into his humble little room where he said his night prayer, after which he sat down to a folio-sized book to read and study. The midnight hour was not far, the children all have slept soundly, and the wife, too, had closed her eyes in slumber, R. Pinchas alone was awake, engaged in deep meditation over some Talmudic passage, when, at a sudden, the little window in his room was tore open with such rashness that its panes clashed, and a chorus of voices shrieked out in the air, at the same time an ugly-looking creature flew in and fell down at his feet. Pinchas sprang from his seat terrorized, calling on God for help, thinking that it was some unclean spirits that visited his abode. He muttered some rabbinic prayers, composed for the banishment of such spirits, ere he would even venture to approach the object that lay motionless on the floor. His wife heard this unusual noise and the low mutterings of her husband, and she ran in to him to see what was the matter, when both of them took courage to look at the corpse that lay dead—it was a dead monkey. R. Pinchas knew enough to discern a monkey from a human being, but he had a false conception of these animals. He thought them to be semi-human, whom the Christians try to civilize, and this idea inspired him with fear and sorrow. It led his mind back to times, as he read, when the Hebrews were persecuted, and as they were often falsely accused of deeds they have not committed so as to get cause to tyrannize them, and he moaned: "O God! now they will come and accuse me and my brethren of a horri-

ble deed we have not committed, and torture us
innocently. Mayest thou, O God, have mercy
upon us." But though he was religious and pious,
he believed that besides prayer activity is needed,
and he now began to ponder what to do; after
various deliberations, the wife proposed to burn
this body and leave no trace of it. This seemed
sound advice, and soon the oven was filled with a
roaring fire. The two lifted the carcass to carry
it to the crematory, when a ringing of a falling
coin startled them, and dropping the ape they
began to search. Imagine the joy when they
found a double ducat (about $4.80), and now they
lifted the dead ape with renewed energy, but this
time one coin began to fall after another. Once
more the carcass was laid down; but this time it
was decided to search whence the coins came, and
it was discovered that they came from the jaws.
A knife was brought and the body opened, and lo,
and behold! its stomach was filled with gold
ducats. R. Pinchas raised his eyes heavenward,
and in the words of David said: "1 have been
young and also grew old, but I hàve not seen the
just forsaken, nor his children begging for bread"
(Psalm xxxvii. 25), and after a prayer of thanksgiving he woke up all the children and showed
them the wonders of God and His timely help,
whereafter the ape was cremated into ashes, leaving no sign or trace of it.

Next day R. Pinchas got himself a fine holiday
suit, and his wife and the children were also
clothed elegantly. *Matzos* and wine were bought,

and other eatables procured; in short the pantry
was filled up and the Passover evening was
ushered in at the humble abode of R. Pinchas
with abundance and sufficiency. The table was
elegantly decorated and the family sat around the
table with glad hearts and merry countenances.

The *sedar* (family service held in every Jewish
house on Passover nights) was just to begin when
a carriage was heard rolling in the street and
stopped before the humble little dwelling of R.
Pinchas. Terror and fright seized upon poor
Pinchas, and the family looked at one another in
silent fear. What does that mean? Who may be
in that carriage? Hark!—some one raps. Pinchas
slowly crept to the door and in quivering voice
asked who was there. He heaved a sigh of relief
when he recognized the voice of the count asking
to be admitted. The door was quickly opened,
and all welcomed the count with reverence and
cordiality.

The generous count had no rest after Pinchas
had left him. His conscience told him that he did
wrong in not extending the usual help to the poor
Jew, and he came to see how poor Pinchas was
faring and his family, in order to appease his want.
No sooner had he entered than Pinchas called all
present to do homage to the " Angel of God," as
he expressed it, and the noble count was ushered
into the family service room.

" Pinchas," said he, " I came here to celebrate
the Passover with you and ask simultaneously
what you are in need of, but from what I can see

you have a great abundance of all and everything, and you and your family are attired in new and elegant clothes. Can it be possible that you became suddenly rich?"

"Yes, my lord!" replied the Hebrew with a pleasing countenance. "God the Almighty had helped me! Yesterday I was poor and in penury, to-day I am rich. Ay, God's help came suddenly, and I will tell you how. I know you feel interested in me. I know that God hath appointed you to be my guardian angel, hence I tell you all," and he related to him the last night's affair with all its details. It turned out to the amazement of both that the ape belonged to the count. He had a bag of gold in his room of which he tried some whether they were genuine, and the monkey, no doubt, thought that he was eating them and no sooner had the count left the room than the ape, imitating his master, ate the golden ducats, filling up his stomach, which killed him dead. The count, on returning, finding the animal dead, ordered its removal from the premises, and the servant with an associate, out of mere fun, took it to the house of Pinchas. They tore open the window and slung the dead animal into the room, accompanied by a chorus of shrieks and laughter. This it was that terrified poor Pinchas, and their voices he took for evil spirits. Next day the count found his ducats missing, accused the servant of stealing them and sent him to prison, where he at this time was; and the count was delighted to hear of the innocence of his servant, which was proven by the monkey being filled with gold. After Pinchas heard this explanation, he arose from his seat and silently stepped to a chest, unlocking it, and took from it a small bag which he handed to the count.

"My lord," said he, "here is your money, all as it came into my possession, except that which I have spent, thinking it my own, for the glorification of our Lord and to appease our want." The count shook his head and refused to accept it, but Pinchas was uneasy and still held it before the count, declaring that the ape was his, the money was his, and consequently should accept it; but the count said, "Nay, Pinchas, God had helped you, and far be it from me to take away from you that which it seems that Providence destined to be yours. Keep it, both for your trust in God and for your honesty. And now, Pinchas, do me the favor and wait awhile with your service till we can bring here the countess, my wife;" and the carriage sped away, soon returning with that distinguished lady; and Pinchas had to say the *sedar* word by word, to which this prominent Christian couple listened ardently and even joined in some hilarity. After the jubilant ceremony was over, the count and the countess departed pleased and delighted.

R. Pinchas after this rose in prominence and riches. His house was the gathering of wise men, his charity and benevolence knew no creed, and he built almost an entire street of houses, which he gave away to homeless poor people. This street exists to this day in the city of Prague, and is known by the name of *Pinchas-Gasse*.

—*Midr. Tanch.* 97 *col.* 3 *and Kav Hajashar* 10.

ALL'S WELL THAT ENDS WELL.

In times long gone by, there lived a wise man whose name was Rabbi Elchanan. He had a pious wife and an only daughter to share the immense riches he was possessor of. How happy they were when their beloved Hannah was led to the matrimonial altar can be well imagined, but, ah! this happiness was of a stillborn character, for the self same night the *Malach hamoves* (the angel of death) visited the abode of Elchanan, to take the life of his son-in-law, and the bride of yesterday was a widow to-day! It was sad, terrible sad! but time is a wonderful curative, and in this instance it was no exception. It was not the exclusive desire of Hannah to be led to the altar again, but the parents so desired it, and she, ever consulting the parents' wishes, again consented to marry, and again she was made a wife. But, alas! the second husband shared the same fate as the first. He, too, was taken by that terrible messenger on his wedding night, and poor Hannah, she was no wife yet and twice a widow. Time again passed, and the parents once more meditated to procure their beloved daughter a protector after they shall have gone, and with all the protests on Hannah's part they once more prevailed; and Hannah once more became the affianced of a man.

The wedding day has arrived and the happy ceremony consummated, but, horror! O horror!
what a doom hung around her! The *Malach hamoves* again visited them and took her husband's
life, and for the third time Hannah became a
widow on her wedding night! She felt as if she
had been guilty of murder, and prayed to God
most devoutly for mercy, expressing her willingness to remain single all the days of her lifetime.

Rabbi Elchanan had a brother, somewhere in
the wide world, where he knew not. They both
had left their homes when yet very young and in
sore want, to find in strange lands a better existence.
Elchanan, as we already know, was fortunate and
became exceedingly rich, but his brother remained
still very poor, scarcely able to give enough
bread for his large family.

One day, after the little children retired hungry,
crying themselves to sleep, the oldest son walked
out into the dark night to air his thoughts and
offer up a prayer to God unheard by human ears,
and he meditated upon his unfortunate position.
It became to him too bitter and oppressive, and
he wept silently, fleeing to God for help, when he
was interrupted by the mysterious and sudden appearance of an old man, who gently placed his hand
on his head, speaking these comforting words:
"O child, weep not, dry thy tears. Knowest
thou not that thou hast a rich uncle, who would be
but too glad and happy to see thee, and give thee
all the aid necessary? Get thee, therefore, on thy
way and seek out thy rich uncle."

He described to him the way to go, and the place to find, and he disappeared as suddenly as he came. The youth at first was astounded, but he soon recovered from his surprise, and went in to his parents, telling them what he had seen and heard, and expressed his desire to depart next day to seek his rich uncle. The parents begged him to desist from his fallacious anticipation, de claring it but an illusion, but all dissuasions fell heedless on his ears, and early next morning already, under sobs, sighs, and tears, he departed, taking along on his journey nothing but the fervent blessing of his beloved father and fond mother. Guided and guarded by this blessing, he journeyed safely till he reached the city and residence of his uncle. The joy of Elchanan was boundless when the youth introduced himself as his brother's son. Tears of joy flowed from all eyes, and on learning the destitute condition of his brother, he forthwith commissioned a faithful servant to take to his brother a sufficiency of everything, and ascertain what more is wanted; but Joseph was kept there and permitted to leave them no more. His modesty and excellent character soon won him the admiration of all, and he was a beloved member of Elchanan's family.

Time passed on and past events were but faint recollections, when one day Joseph entered the presence of his uncle, expressing desire to speak with him on a subject of great importance. The uncle looked at his nephew with admiration, and was willing to listen to all he wanted to say.

" Dear uncle," began he, " you have received me kindly, nobly, and the kindness you heap upon me daily emboldens me to ask a great favor of you, trusting that you will not refuse to grant it."

" Refuse you a favor?" exclaimed the uncle, "no favor, however, great would I refuse you, my son. Speak, what shall it be?"

"Nay, dear uncle," reiterated Joseph, "the favor is too great, and I fear to ask it, except you would swear that you would grant it."

" I know," said R. Elchanan, " that you would not ask for anything impossible, nor for anything that is wrong and I swear that I will grant it if I only can ;" but he sprang horror-struck to his feet, when Joseph asked for the hand of Hannah, his daughter.

" O my dear son," moaned the uncle, "do not ask that. Thou knowest well that three men have lost their lives as her husbands, and, oh, how dearly I and we love you ; may you not share the the same fate? Ask for riches, wealth, and for all treasures I possess—ask for all that I have, but, pray, desist from that desire." " Dearest uncle, I cannot !" emphatically declared Joseph. " I knew your emotions and therefore I caused you to swear. There is no riches and no wealth that could make me happy without Hannah, and whatever transpired in the great past will not make me shrink, trusting in God that all will end well. The uncle, seeing that all his efforts and dissuasions could not move Joseph from his anticipations, he called for Hannah, apprising her of this, and she began to weep and plead with Joseph; but this made matters only worse, for this convinced Joseph that Hannah loved him in return, and he was inflexible.

Bound by his oath, Elchanan finally yielded, and the day was set when Joseph and Hannah were to be wedded. The poor bride spent most of her time in seclusion, praying to God most fervently that, if it was His sacred will that her intended shall die, He should take her instead, that she shall no more bring such precious sacrifice. As to Joseph, he was the object of pity, for all learned to love him, and all prayed for him. He was the true friend to the poor, and the pleasant companion to the ch.

The day of the wedding has at last arrived, and the guests assembled to witness the ceremony and to see their friends united. Hannah was to be led to the altar, and Joseph stood already at the side of the *chuppah* (a canopy used, in the orthodox ritual, as a matrimonial altar) to step under it at the appearance of the bride, when a poor man approached him asking for aid. Joseph, even at this moment, evaded not the mendicant, but was generous and charitable to him; but no sooner had he given him his bountiful alm than he recognized him, on the words of blessing he uttered, as the same old man that appeared to him in his day of trouble, advising him to seek his rich uncle. He knew that it must have been Elijah,* the prophet. After the

---

* Tradition has it that Elijah still wanders on earth and can make himself visible or invisible, or appear in any shape or form at many

ceremony, the numerous guests were seated at tables decked with dainties and refreshments of the highest order, of which rich and poor partook alike. The most remarkable incident was the appearance of a beggar clad in the poorest garb, whom Joseph nevertheless treated with cordiality.

The feast was already over, and the bride had retired, and Joseph, too, intended to retire, when this beggar followed him and whispered faintly unto him: "Get thee to thy chamber, for I am the *malach hamoves* sent to take thy life. Now prepare to die!" Joseph reached his chamber and there turned to this black messenger: "Oh, grant me one week time to prepare! I pray thee!" "I am very sory," said the destroyer, "but I must obey orders and can extend no more time than necessary to die." "Let me then, I pray thee, take leave of my wife?" "As thou wert kind to me," said the *malach hamoves*, "I will grant thee this favor," and Joseph repaired to Hannah's apartment. He found her immersed in prayer, and when she beheld him, she leaped up for joy and embraced him in her arms, but Joseph informed her that he came to bid her good-by forever: "I, too, am doomed," moaned he, "the horrible messenger granted me just time to take leave of thee, and he is waiting for me." "My husband!" she shrieked, "if thou goest, I go with thee! Where thou shalt die, I shall die! Alone thou wilt not go!" And seeing the angel of death, she ap-

---

places simultaneously; and to whom he appears must be worthy, and he always brings tidings of salvation.

proached him: "Scriptures say that 'if a man taketh a wife, he shall for a year not go to war,' etc. (Deut. xxiv. 15), and thou wouldst take away a man just wedded, heedless of God's own law?" "Thou art a pious woman and speakest words of wisdom," replied the *malach hamoves*. "'The law of God is perfect' (Psalm xix. 19). I will ascend to heaven in your behalves and plead for the charitable Joseph and the pious Hannah." And away he flew. As he did not return, it became evident to them that it must have pleased the Lord to change His decree from death to life, even as it is written in Solomon's Proverbials (x. 2): "Charity redeems from death." And Joseph with Hannah lived a long and happy life.

CHARITY KNOWS NO CREED.

A poor man was once wandering through the streets in a most unhappy mood, in quest of some necessaries of life. It was Friday, with no prospect of getting something to eat for his family on the Sabbath. Every baker and butcher he visited, begging to be trusted with some bread and meat, promising faithfully to pay for it next week, but none wanted to trust him with the smallest amount. Joseph, the *traifener katzev*,* saw the poor man passing and repassing the streets, and noticing his embarrassment, asked him: "Rab Moshe, what's the matter? You look so down-hearted." "Well, what's the use to tell you, you can't help me anyway." "Why not? Am I not a man like anybody else," said, Joseph, "even if I am not as devout an Israelite as far as outward manifestations concern? Or can *no* man help you?" "I want some bread and meat for *shabbos*,"† said R. Moshe, but, having no money for it, nobody wants to trust me; but you sell *traife*‡ me t anyway, so from you I wouldn't take it, even were you to give it to me." "Well, Rab Moshe, come here," said the butcher in a kind-hearted manner, "I have here a beautiful

---

* A butcher selling meat of cattle slain not in accordance with rab-binic law.

† Sabbath.   ‡ Unclean.

hide which you will have no trouble to sell, and at a good price, too, I believe; take it, sell it, buy bread, meat, and flour, too, and the remainder you can keep for next week to *schacher** with. Tell your wife to make a good *Kugel.*†

Rab Moshe, with the assistance of Joseph, lifted the hide on his shoulder, and skipped away on his toes to the *wochenmarkt,*‡ and had really no trouble in selling the hide, just as Joseph said. Imagine the joy of the darling children, when the father came home, and when they asked for bread, that they could get all they wanted to eat of it, a thing that seldom happened. He then produced a fine *berches*§ and plenty of meat, flour and other victuals, besides handing his wife a few thalers for safe keeping until he could go out to business.

The family of Rab Moshe had a *shabbos, wer mir gut's goennt.*‖ Next Monday he went out with the balance of the money he got for the hide, and the maxim, " Der Groschen is suess, der mit *chazir* beschmiert ist,¶ seemed to have been verified, as Rab Moshe had luck with it. He began to earn money fast with it, and was soon in pleasant circum-

---

* To trade. This word probably derives from the Hebrew *shachar*, to hire, to reward, etc.

† Pudding.

‡ A market held once a week, as is customary in European cities.

§ A fine bread expressly baked for sabbath or holidays, so called from the word *b'racha*, blessing, as the bread is cut open by saying grace.

‖ Who wishes me well shall have it.

¶ That groschen is sweet that is smeared with lard, meaning that comes from a non-Jew, or non-observant Jew.

stances, paying Joseph for the hide with grateful acknowledgment, and never again did he have such a miserable Friday.

.   .   .   .

Many years have elapsed since then. Rab Moshe was already sleeping the sleep that knows no waking, when Joseph too had been summoned away from the land of the living.

He was taken before the Great Tribunal, to answer to the indictments pending against him. Gabriel stood there holding up in his left hand a scale, and with his right he placed into one side indictment after indictment. Joseph stood trembling and terror struck, awaiting the terrible sentence. He was asked what he had to say to the indictment of selling *traife* meat. His answer was far insufficient to justify him, much less acquit him, and the indictment was handed to Gabriel, whose charge it was to place it in the scale. Another indictment was taken up, and Joseph was again asked what he had to say to the charge of violating the Sabbath, and this indictment was consigned into the same scale as the first. Indictment after indictment was taken up in the same manner, and disposed of likewise. One side of the scale, which Gabriel held up high was now balanced down as down it could go, it contained the demerits of Joseph ; and now the meritorious briefs were taken up, but they were far too light to outbalance the indictments, and the Great Judge was about to pronounce sentence, when from a distance he beheld one hurrying as fast as he could towards the place of judgment, with a big heavy hide on his back. The allwise and alljust Judge waited a while to see if, perchance, it might be something in favor of the transgressor, and so it was. For it was Rab Moshe that came running with the hide Joseph had given him on that memorable Friday when his family needed bread and pious people refused to trust him; while Joseph, without having been asked, offered the help unsolicited, and after which a family became self-sustaining.

On the hide itself was nothing written, of course not, but its history was recorded in a great, great book, which was called for and read, and the hide was thrown into the scale containing the merits of Joseph. Imagine, dear reader, how it outbalanced the demerits. Sentence was suspended, and Rab Moshe was entrusted with the charge to lead Joseph, the traifener katzev, into *gan eden* (Paradise), where they live together in eternal life as neighbors never to part.

—Oral tradition.

THE TRUE RELIGION.

A heathen once came to Shamai, and said,
" Rabbi, pray tell me wherein consists thy religion?
"Study our oral and written law, and you will
find it out," answered the Hebrew sage. " In
oral law," said the Heathen, " I have no faith, but
if you could teach me your written law, and that
within the time that I could stand on one foot, I
would embrace your religion." Shamai drove
him off with a cane he had in his hand, and the
Heathen went before Hillel, in like manner.
Hillel complacently told him to stand on his foot,
and while the Heathen thus stood, he significantly
said, " Do not unto others what should displease
thee, if others did it to thee. This is the whole
substance, all the rest is commentary. Now go
and study."

—Sab. 31, *a.*

Lessing, the German poet, an intimate friend of
Moses Mendelssohn, gives in his " Nathan der
Weise," to Saladin a beautiful illustration of the
true religion in the following manner:

There lived in ancient times a wise man, who
was father of three sons. He had a family relic, a
ring, that was supposed to possess the charm of
making the holder beloved before God and man,
if he believed in its virtues.

He intended to leave this relic to the son he loved best, but years glided by and the wise father could make no proper disposition of it, as he loved all three sons alike. One day, as he was reflecting upon the time when he should have to end his pilgrimage on the terrestrial sphere, he began to meditate earnestly. Should he give the ring to one, and slight the others? For that he was too just, and too fond a parent. He concluded on a happy plan, which he executed at once.

He visited a skilful mechanic, and had two rings made exactly like the genuine. When, one day, he felt that his last hour was approaching, he called his sons, each separately, to his bedside, declaring to each his love and paternal affection; and giving him a ring, with his last admonition and blessing, he expired.

For a while the sons were too deeply imbued with the sad loss they had sustained, and all went on as before; but soon one of the sons, thinking himself to be the favored inheritor of the family relic, endeavored to show mastery over the others. They, however, arose in protest, each claiming the same recipiency, and to settle the matter they went before a judge. Each gave evidence of having received the ring from the father, and the judge was so perplexed that he was at a loss how to decide the case.

"I understood you to say," said he after a brief ponder, "that the genuine ring possesses the charm of making the holder beloved and appreciable before God and man; now, let me see the ring manifest its virtue. Which of you shall be most beloved?" All three were silent. "Now," continued the judge, "may you not appear deceived deceivers? May not your father have three rings made like the one genuine? And might he not have done so to show you each equal love? What matters it, then, which is the genuine as long as you have received the ring from your father, if you revere the father? Retire, therefore, and live in peace, esteeming each your rings as a token of your father's love, and wait till their charm shall work."

This ring is religion; each and every one believes that he has the true religion; and each and every one believes to have received it from his (heavenly) Father. If so, then hold it sacred as such, and the one that can make you beloved before God and man is the true religion. Why, every religion can do that if you live up to it; so then is every religion a gift from God who, to show us His love to all equally, reveals not to us His preference, for " Have we not all one Father? hath not one God created us?" said Malachi the Prophet.

Ephraim ben Sancho, a learned Hebrew, was once arraigned before Don Pedro, of Aragon, to explain which is the best religion, and he answered: " Mine is the best to me, for the Holy One, blessed be He, who redeemed my ancestors from Egyptian bondage, gave it them; but to thee, O king, the Christian must needs be the best, as God endowed

thy people with power and civilization." This
was, however, unsatisfactory to the monarch, and
he demanded proof more convincing, under threats
of severe punishment should he be unable to produce it. The Hebrew sage begged a day's time
for meditation, which was readily granted.

The following morning Ephraim sought the
presence of the king, filled with anxiety and in
apparent forgetfulness of the important explanation he was to give, he clamored for justice in a
certain matter. "What matter is that?" asked
Don Pedro. "Some time ago," related the Hebrew, "my neighbor departed for a journey, leaving to each of his two sons a costly jewel; but no
sooner was the parent gone, than the sons began
to dispute regarding the intrinsic value of their
respective jewels. Yesterday, they sought my
opinion, and I told them the donor was the best
judge, and that they should cease quarrelling. I
advised them to wait peacefully till their father
should return or they go to him, and, instead of
accepting my advice, they fell upon me and beat
me. Have I deserved such treatment for my
counsel?"

"No," said the king, "thy advice seems correct,
and they shall be punished for this offence."

"Sire!" resumed the complainant in accents of
humbleness, "pardon me for referring to the
words that have just now escaped thy lips: Esau
and Jacob were brothers, and each of them received a costly jewel—*religion*—from their Father
who is in heaven; and to ask which is the better

of the two is equal to your inquiry of yesterday, when you threatened me with torture in case I were unable to advance convincing argument. My advice to the two brothers, my lord, you have just now pronounced correct. I, therefore, will repeat the same advice to you. Wait till we should appear before Him who gave us our religion. He alone knows the true value of our faith." The Hebrew was excused.

—*M. Nissim.*

WHILE THERE IS LIFE THERE IS HOPE.

There lived once a rich miser who mercilessly denied every assistance to his fellow-creatures however destitute and needy they were, and he himself enjoyed not the life his wealth could afford him. One day, as he was looking over his hoarded up pelf, a deep thought came over him—after all, what good have I from this gold? I, too, will have to die and leave this for others to enjoy. At this moment an old man appeared before him, and admonishingly told him that this wealth was a blessing from God and he should aid the sufferer and help the poor. "Ah!" exclaimed the miser, with a frown on his countenance, "I will take thy advice, and give my hard-earned money to such who need it; however, very careful will I be to whom I shall give, surely not to any mendicant. I *swear* to give but to such sufferer who abandoned all hope for terrestial life." And his former deep thought returned no more, for his heart was mercilessly closed as ever before, blind, deaf, and heedless to all misery and suffering of others. One day, while walking in a street, his gaze met an object of the greatest pity his eyes ever beheld. A human being lay there, yet hardly breathing, so faint and weak that every moment his life might have become extinct.   He stepped to the sufferer, drew forth a few gold coins, and extended it to the poor man.   "O God!" faintly moaned the unfortunate man, "have my hopes at last become realized?   Shall at last my misery have ended?   And thou, O noble man, becomest my savior! pray, whereby have I deserved this from thy bounty?"   "I swore," explained the miser, "that I will help only such who have abandoned all hope of earthly life, and I find thee in such condition that thou canst not live long, and I will fulfil my my oath."   Like supported by an invisible hand the sick man erected himself, and with the little strength he could muster he began: "O thou fool! thou it is who hast given up the hope to live, for thou livest not.   Thou only breathest the life of thy perishable treasures!"   Surprised at this harsh admonition, the rich miser said, "Is this what thou givest me for my willingness to help thee?" "Nay!" replied the sick man, "I take not thy help, for my hope has not yet forsaken me, notwithstanding my abject misery and destitute condition.   Only the already dead can cease to hope." Away walked the miser, thinking shall he ever be able to fulfil his oath.   To the graveyard he went; he dug a hole near a grave, took the coins and deposited them there, muttering, "Here, then, O dead, it is to thee only that I can offer the fulfilment of my oath.' . . .

Time passed by, the rich miser became poor, unforeseen misfortunes have so reduced him that he became a helpless wanderer in the wide world.

Oh, how often did he reproach himself, " Would I
have but lived for my money! None have I
helped, and none helps me! Many a person have
I harmed and wronged in obtaining his money,
and for what? what have I now?" All such bitter recollections pressed upon his memory. After
many years of homelessness he once more returned
to his native city in greater destitution than ever.
He thought of the money he buried in the graveyard, and to save him from starvation he went to
the grave and began to dig for it, when the watch-
man arrested and brought him before the judge.
"How darest thou to molest our graves and the
dead?" asked the judge harshly. "O judge, hear
my plea!" cried the once rich miser, "it is not the
dead nor the graves that I wished to molest; but
I once was rich, and I never gave to the poor; and
would never have given, but owing to an old
man's admonition, I *swore* that I would help such
who hope no more to live, and as I could find none
to be so hopeless, I buried some money in the
graveyard near a grave; and now that I am in the
deepest destitution, I wished to dig that money up
for bread." He gave the judge his whole life's
history, and to find whether he spoke the truth,
the judge sent for that money, which was really
found, thus establishing the truthfulness of his tale.
The judge then addressed the penitent miser: "I
find that thou hast told me the truth, and I will
assuredly help thee. I will also convince thee,
however, that thou hast grossly erred, by telling
thee that I am that man whom thou hast once

found in such pitiful condition ; with hope still sparkling in his breast, when thou hast thought that his life was beyond hope. I am here alive, well, and well-to-do. Be this a lesson to thee, that while there is life there is hope."

—*Simchath nefesh*, 21.

ELIEZER BEN HYRKANUS.

Several miles from Jerusalem, there lived a wealthy farmer by the name of Hyrkanus. He was father of several children, all devoted to the toil of the fields and vineyards. One of them, however, seemed to become recreant to his duties as farmer, and expressed his dissatisfaction, giving vent to grief and melancholiness. One day the father, as usual, came out in the fields to see his sons, and noticed the despondency of Eliezer. Thinking that the share of work allotted to him was the cause, he promoted the youth to a higher sphere of labor; but he continued in his despondency and grew day by day sadder. The father at last inquired of his son, "Eliezer, what aileth thee? Tell me if thy avocation is unpleasant, or too hard, and I will change or obtain thee an employment more agreeable."

Instead of answering, however, Eliezer stood in tears before his father. The fond parent pressed for an answer, and was anxious to know the secrecy of his son, who finally found words: " O father, I desire to study!" "To study!" exclaimed Hyrkanus. "To study! now when thou art twenty and eight years old? Take my advice and marry; and have then, with the help of God, thy children to study."

The youth found no words to reply, but became sadder than ever. He hardly took any food, and walked around like a stray sheep. An idea flashed to his mind.* To go to Jerusalem, and to Jerusalem he hied, taking leave from neither father nor brothers. In Jerusalem, he soon found the academy of Ben Zaccay which he entered, but was so abashed that he stood before the great teacher like numb and speechless, with tears coursing down his cheeks. " Why weepest thou, my son ?" addressed him the Rabbi. "I weep," replied Eliezer, because I thirst for knowledge." " Hast thou learned something heretofore ?" inquired the sage. "Nothing! Oh, nothing have I learned!" said Eliezer, moanfully.

The great teacher, noticing Eliezer's yearning desire for learning, took pain to instruct him, and he soon showed his preceptor that his perceptive organs were extraordinary; and the student by degrees rose in talent and learning, so that in a short few years, he numbered among the ablest scholars Ben Zaccay had in his academy.

Meanwhile his brothers, not knowing his whereabouts, denounced him bitterly and decried his behavior as shameful, accusing him of laziness and indolence, so much that his father believed it, and influenced by his sons, he determined to disinherit Eliezer. With this intention, Hyrkanus repaired to Jerusalem, there to arrange his will, and sought his friends, who introduced the wealthy

---

* Tradition wants it that Elijah appeared to him, and gave him advice.

farmer to the chief of the academy, Ben Zaccay. Hyrkanus, descending from a noble ancestry,* was well received, and there being a feast in the house of Zaccay, he was invited to participate among the nobles and the scholars of Jerusalem. Ben Zaccay, desirous to show the talent of Eliezer, besought him, during the progress of the feast, to rise and expound something of the law. But Eliezer in protest responded, "O Rabbi! the cistern can only yield the same water that had been consigned into it, what could I advance that is unknown to thee?"

"My son," exhorted the Rabbi, "a fountain streams forth water continually, yet gets not exhausted," but Eliezer only blushed and kept silent. The tutor, to relieve him of his embarrassment, arose and left the room, and Eliezer began to expound matters of importance with the most profound scholarship, to which all listened ardently; his father, who knew him not, as he underwent such change in appearance and deportment, included. As he concluded his exposition, Rabbi Ben Zaccay rushed into the room, and sprang to Eliezer, embracing him, and pressing a kiss on his forehead, exclaimed: "Blessed art thou, a Hyrkanus' son! Happy can Israel be to have such masters amongst them!" The father sprang to his feet and in amazement asked, "Of whom didst thou say this, O master?" and Zaccay answered, "Of thy son, who stands at thy side." At this the father recognized his son, and clasped him to his

---

* From Jochanan Hyrkanus, the high-priest.

breast with words of affection and pateral emo-
tion. It is useless to say that he did not disinherit his son, of whom he was proud, and who
became a revered master and teacher in Israel.

—Pirke D'rabbi Eliezer, 4.

THE TWO STRANGERS OF WORMS.

At Worms, on the Rhine, a visitor of the old synagogue cannot fail to notice two lights perpetually burning on two candlesticks on which the words שני אורחים (*sh'nai orchim*)* are engraved. The history of these lights dates back to time immemorial, when the Hebrews lived in the Ghettos. It was once that a festive procession, headed by the bishop, drew through the streets of Worms, and, contrary to the usual custom, they marched this time through the Ghetto. They proceeded not far when, from the top of some of the houses, a liberal share of refuse came pouring down, emptying itself on the unfurled banner of the standard of Catholicism and the bishop himself. This was enough to so infuriate the pilgrims that they fell upon the unfortunate Jews, maltreating them; and soon plunder and pillage of their houses and storerooms would have begun were it not for the just and generous magistrate who, in stern command, bid them to cease their unholy work, and commit no inhuman atrocities. The command was obeyed, but the cry for vengeance rang loud ; the demand for blood was so ferocious that the magistrate could not help demanding a scapegoat. He ordered the Jews to deliver the perpetrator, and

---

* Two visitors, generally strangers.

succeeded in dispersing the mob for twenty-four
hours, in which time the Jews were to produce
the offender.   Alas! alas! who was the offender?
None would confess; none would feel inclined to
deliver himself up to the arm of justice, and a
night of terror and pang was spent.   The morning dawned, and the woe-bestricken Jews assembled in the synagogue, devoutly praying to that
Great Redeemer that had on this self-same day—
being the seventh day of Passover—redeemed
them from Egypt, and led them safely through
the billowy waves of the Red Sea.   And oh, how
fervent were their prayers! The sun rose brightly,
sending forth its lustre, which, to the unfortunate
Hebrews, seemed a tantalizing light.   The tumul-
tuous element renewed their cry for vengeance,
and repaired towards the Ghetto. Nearer and
nearer came the mob, and they already were in
sight of the synagogue calling, " Give us the offender, or woe to you all."   There was very little
time for speech-making, and the rabbi, in touching
remarks, urged the Israelites to be steadfast, and
accept the approaching calamity as a trial of our
faith. " The God," said he, " who delivered on
this very day the Israelites from a mighty Egyptian host, is able to send, if we are worthy and
guiltless, deliverance at the last moment."   At this
time, the mob pressed already into the sanctuary,
with their cry, " Give us the offender!" and, as
the terrified Hebrews stood with no offender to
deliver, and, just as the ringleader gave the command of attack, and the Israelites commending

themselves to God with loud SHMA YISROEL'S,* two hoary-headed, giant-like men pressed through the .throng, and shouted a commanding "Halt!" They were so taken by surprise that all became silenced, and one of the two strangers began : " Touch not the innocent, for we are the guilty ones, and we deliver ourselves into your hands!" A moment more, and the two strangers were hurled into the crowd, dragged out, a pyre was erected, and the two martyrs thrown in. This appeased the wrath of the mob, and quiet was restored. Who these men were, whence they came, and what were their names, none knew, nor could it ever be ascertained. Suffice it that they have saved the Israelites of Worms from calamity, wherefore the congregation, in their memory, had two candlesticks made, and placed near the ark, keeping the candles they hold perpetually burning, and, in representation of their names, " SH'NAI OR-CHIM " was engraven on them.

—*Maase Nissim*, 3.

---

* Hear, O Israel, the Lord is our God, the Lord is One !—Deut. vi. 4. This is a motto adopted by Israelites as a confession of faith, and they are the last words of a dying Jew. If he can speak no more, those attending speak it. Hence, when danger threatens, Israelites find it natural to exclaim SHMA YISROEL !

HILLEL'S PATIENCE.

Who has not heard of Hillel? He lived about half a century before the Christian era, and was the principal of a rabbinical seminary, and the head of another high school at Jerusalem. His generous principles were equal to his liberality in views, and only excelled by his patience, which, among Israelites, is a maxim yet this day. Not unfrequently it is heard, if some one is calm and patient, "*Der hat Hillel's Geduld*" (he has the patience of Hillel). So, among the vast illustrations of his patience, one anecdote is related, that a spirited youth once, hearing praised the patience of Hillel, offered a bet that he could provoke and break his patience. He carefully sought the opportunity, and seeing, one Friday, Hillel entering a bath-room, he thought it the best chance, and he began to call, without any prefix of title whatever, "Hillel! O Hillel! is Hillel here?" "I am here," replied Hillel, and stepped out of the water, wrapping himself in a mantle, and went to meet the young man. "What desirest thou, my son?" asked he sweetly. "I have a question to ask," said the young man, "if you will allow me." "Ask, my son, ask," said Hillel. "Why," asked the youth, "have Babylonians peaked heads?" "Ah," said Hillel, not to discourage him; "thou hast

asked a good question. It is because they have
no efficient midwives." The young man departed
without ceremony or salute, and Hillel returned to
his bath; but no sooner was he in the water, when
the youth called again : " Hillel! O Hillel! Is Hillel here ? " " I am here," answered Hillel again ;
and again wrapping himself up, he stepped out to
the young man, and pleasantly asked him : " What
desirest thou, my son ? " " I have a question to
ask thee," replied the youth. " Ask, my son," said
Hillel. " Why," asked the youth, " have the Ther-
modians weak eyes ? " Hillel, as before, encouraged
him that it was a great question he had asked, and
told him that it was because they lived in sandy
regions. The young man again departed, and
Hillel stepped back into his bath. But scarcely
was he in the water when the same voice rang
out in the same manner: " Hillel! O Hillel! is
Hillel here ? " And Hillel, as if it was for the first
time he was called, stepped out again, and went to
meet the youth. " I am here, my son; what desirest thou ? " asked he, without showing the slightest provocation. " I have a question to ask thee,"
said the youth. " Ask, my son, ask," responded
Hillel, and the youth asked: " Why have all
Africans wide feet ? " Hillel, in the same expression as before," answered : " Because they live
in swampy regions." " Oh, I had some more questions to ask of thee," said the young man, " but I
fear I might provoke thee." Hillel, drawing his
mantle closer, and seating himself, said : " My
son, ask all the questions thou desirest to ask ; fear

not." "Art thou that Hillel," inquired the youth, "whom they call the Nassi (prince) in Israel?" "I am he," replied Hillel. "I wish," said the young man, "that there should not be many like thee in Israel." "Why not?" asked Hillel, not even in a voice of astonishment. "Because," replied the youth, "I have lost four hundred zuzim (certain silver coins) on account of thee. I bet that I could provoke thee to anger." "Ah, my son," said Hillel, in sweet admonition; "beware of thy spirit! It is far better that thou lose four hundred zuzim than Hillel should lose his patience."

—*Sabbath*, 31 *a.*

To this can be compared the mild disposition of Sir Isaac Newton. It is related that he had a little dog named Diamond, and on one occasion Mr. Newton was called out of his study to an adjoining apartment, when the little dog threw down a lighted lamp among his papers, and the almost finished labors of many years were consumed in a few moments. Sir Newton, on his returning, beheld, with great mortification, his irreparable loss; but he only exclaimed, with his usual self-possession: "*O Diamond! Diamond!* thou little knowest the mischief thou hast done."

RASHI.*

This great commentator on Scripture and Talmud was born in Troyes, France, in 1040, and
studied under the tuition of Rabbenu Gershon,
acquiring unlimited knowledge of all literature
then attainable, among which branches Jewish
theology, as well as Greek and Arabian classics,
were the objects of his indefatigable researches.

His commentaries upon the Pentateuch stand
unexcelled in brevity, diction, and clearness.

Though fierce and fiery in defense of Judaism
and truth, meekness and modesty marked his demeanor.

Travelling once in the Orient, it so happened
that a monk travelled the same road, and a conversation ensued exchanging their ideas. However liberal Rashi's advancements were, the monk
was inclined to be otherwise, for he soon began to
fiercely attack his companion's religion, which
brought forth the most earnest debates on the part
of Rashi; but the monk became intolerant and
defiant, and the two divines, on reaching an inn,
were not as friendly as when they started on the
journey together. While in the inn the priest

---

* He was called so from the initials of his real name רבי שלמה
יצחקי *Rabbi Salomoh Yitzchaki.* This was customary among Hebrews. Their scholars were all called by such abbreviated names.

took suddenly sick, and physicians were summoned
to his assistance. They treated him awhile, but
soon pronounced his malady mortal, and Rashi on
hearing this repaired to his bedside. Examining
him carefully, he prepared a medicine which he
administered, and otherwise nursed his antagonist with fraternal kindness, and the priest's health
was restored. The monk, having learned this,
wished to express his gratitude to his benefactor,
but Rashi interrupted him with the words, "You
owe me no thanks. I have only done my duty, for,
though divided in faith, we must still be united by
that love of mankind which Moses enjoined on us,
'Love thy neighbor as thyself' (Lev. xix. 18). I
simply beg of you, should you ever meet a suffering Hebrew, help him as I have helped you. Farewell!" and he departed.

Several years thereafter Rashi visited Prague,
and was received by the Jewish populace with
great distinction and marked reverence. Duke
Wladislow, who was then elector, hated the Jews
most bitterly, and never failed to manifest his
hatred at every possible opportunity. On hearing
of Rashi's reception, he begrudged even that delight of the Jews, and to crush the pre-eminent
standing of Rashi, had him arrested, branding him
with no less a crime than spyism. All interces-
sions were of no avail, and evidence to the contrary
could, so hastily, not be produced, and Wladislow
was about to pronounce sentence of death as a matter of course, when the Bishop of Olmutz stepped
before the tribunal, exclaiming: " In the name of

God will I protect and defend this Jew! He can be no spy! One that is so faithful to the laws of God, and has such noble and generous heart as this man has, can be no spy!" It was that monk whom Rashi once so kindly nursed when they had travelled together; he was afterwards promoted to the bishopric. He related this to the duke with all the incidents connected with it, and Wladislow, in pleasing surprise, became calm, his prejudicate opinion of Jews changed, and conferred himself upon Rashi many honors and distinctions. The noble Hebrew embraced this opportunity, and appealed to the now kind duke in behalf of his brethren, securing them thereafter shelter and protection in Prague. After a life most noble, and a caree. most virtuous, Rashi died in Troyes, his native place, in 1105.

—Post-Biblical History of the Jews.

MAN'S THREE FRIENDS.

A certain man had three friends. One was the love of his admiration—in his avocation as in his pleasure, in his parlor and in his dining-room this friend was with him. At home and abroad this friend occupied his mind—his dreams were filled with this friend. The second friend he also loved, yet not with such ardency as his first; the third, however, he loved least. If it so happened that they perchance have met, he recognized him very friendly, but it was once in a great while he would go to see him, and that out of mere courtesy, while to his own house he would seldom, if ever, invite him. One day, as it happened, the king summoned him to appear without delay; and, conscience-stricken, he hastened to his first and dearest friend, begging him to go with him before the king, and speak for him if necessary; but the friend indifferently replied: "I cannot go with thee. I know not the king nor does he know me, and I have no influence with him whatsoever; besides, I cannot leave my affairs to go with thee." Entreaties, supplications, and tears, all were of no avail—the friend was immovable. Disheartened and grief-stricken, he ran to his second friend and solicited his kindness to go with him before the king, but he replied, somewhat regretfully: "I feel very

much pained that I cannot go with thee, although
I would like to help thee; but I will go with thee
as far as the gate, and thence thou hast to go alone."
Dispirited and dejected, he went to his third friend,
who listened to him attentively and extended his
arms to embrace him, speaking to him most cordially: "How glad I am that I can be serviceable
to thee, my friend! Thou canst not imagine how
I love thee and how I waited for an opportunity
to show thee my kindness! I know the king well
and I will go with thee into his presence; I will
plead for thee if necessary, and I feel certain that
I will obtain his favor in thy behalf." These three
friends are *wealth*, *relatives*, and *religion*; the summons is the death-call, and the king is the Holy
One, blessed be He.

Wealth it is that we so dearly love; for that,
peace and rest are sacrificed. Our houses are the
strongest reminders of it; we toil for it and dream
of it. Relatives we love next; but how often are
they neglected, especially if they need our help;
but Religion is the friend we love the least. Once
in a great while some will go to the house of religious instruction and prayer, and that because it
is fashion, or some other necessity requires it; but
to our houses we seldom invite it, that is, we seldom
participate in religious practices. Suddenly, the
King of kings sends His summons—the death call
—and we appeal to our Mammon, to our wealth
and accumulations, in vain, for they will cruelly
and disdainfully forsake us. They have no influence with the King, nor would they be able to

obtain you even the shortest respite. They remain here and we have to go.   Our relatives they weep and cry and would like to help us, but they cannot. They can come with us to the gate—the grave— and thence we have to go alone.   But the third friend—Religion—will always receive us kindly, even at the last moment, if we apply to it.   It will embrace us in its arms and take us before the Infinite King, there plead for us and secure us bliss everlasting.

—Pirke R. Eliezer, 34.

IS LABOR DISGRACEFUL?

Aside of the manifold sublime precepts and doctrines divine that Scriptures contain, they also teach us that labor is not depreciating the estimation of man, however high his position or rank may be. They inform us that Abraham, Isaac, and Jacob—our patriarchs—were shepherds. Moses received his divine message when feeding the flock. David was promoted to the royalty from a shepherd's occupation. King Saul and the prophet Elisha were agriculturists. Israelites were instructed by Moses to become laborers, and they have listened to his instructions. At the time when Nebuchadnezzar conquered Jerusalem, he carried away a thousand smiths and craftsmen (see 2 Kings xxiv. 14–16). Our ancestors gloried in labor, and some of our greatest teachers were laborers. Hillel the great was a woodcutter; Rabbi Joshua, a pinmaker; Rabbi Nehemiah Hackador, a potter; Rabbi Judah, a tailor; Rabbi Joshua Hassandler, a shoemaker; Rabbi Judah Hanechtan, a baker; Rabbi Josai ben Chalafta, a tanner; Rabbi Judah ben Illai Hachasid, a cooper; etc., etc. The most noteworthy of these, however, was Hillel Hannassi, the prince, as he was called. From a woodchopper he became the principal of a famous seminary, and great authority in lore and learning. He was a Babylonian, about forty years old, when he settled in Jerusalem, void of all knowledge and without a trade, he obtained a livelihood by cutting wood. Impelled by an unquenchable yearning for knowledge, he offered his services as woodcutter for poor rabbis for the mere permission of listening to their lectures and teachings. Afterwards he gained admittance into the celebrated academy of Shemaiah and Abtalion; but every student had there to pay a small admission fee for the doorkeeper for the defrayal of expenses of fuel and light which on poor Hillel was very hard. One day he could not earn enough to do this and, anxious not to miss his lesson, he climbed upon the window-sill and there he listened to the lesson inside regardless of the approaching storm. Meanwhile, the snow began to fall, heavier and heavier did it come down, covering him more and more until he was discovered stiff and unconscious. Applications and restoratives brought him to consciousness again, and as the tutors ascertained his great desire for learning and longing for truth, they granted him free admission to their lectures. Fast advancing, Hillel became the revered master; the title Nassi (prince) was conferred upon him, and he was worthy of it, not only on account of his great profundity, but his deportment and manners distinguished him as a true prince.

—Compiled Facts.

A LESSON TO BE TOLERANT.

When Abraham was yet young and unacquainted with the attributes and the holy mission of God's love to all, that noble trait of hospitality was intuitive with him, and as one day he sat in his tent, he espied from far off a man approaching. Nigher and nigher came he, and soon Abraham could discern that it was an old man, and, thinking that the poor traveller might have journeyed a long distance, he ran to meet him and cordially invited him to his tent to tarry awhile and rest from his journey which the weary traveller gladly accepted. Abraham had hastily prepared a meal and brought it to the wayfarer, which was assuredly welcome, as in those days there were no people easily found to treat a stranger so hospitably.

"Eat, I pray thee," said Abraham, " for thou must undoubtedly be hungry." "Ay, my son, I am that," replied the old man. "I am indeed very hungry and I accept thy kindness thankfully;" and he prepared with utter delight to partake of this food. He was about to convey the first morsel to his lips, when Abraham gently tapped him on the shoulder saying, "Bless the Lord, O man, the God from whom all blessing flows ere thou partakest of food. "O young man," replied the stranger, "dost thou indeed believe that there is a God to prepare all things? Why! it is nature that produces all." An argument ensued in which the traveller would not be convinced and Abraham would not be disputed, and he bid the wayfarer to leave his tent.

Presently a soft, sweet voice called, "Abraham, Abraham!" "Here am I," answered Abraham, feeling that it was the voice of God; and he stood in awe and reverence ardently listening to what Ellohim wished to impart to him—and the voice continued, "Where is the man whom thou didst invite to thy tent?"

"O God!" replied Abraham, "he proved to be an unbeliever in Thee, and as no godless man shall tarry beneath my roof, I could not tolerate him and bid him to depart."

" Ah, Abraham!" said the Lord, " I have endured it with him for three score years and ten, I have endowed him with the same health, and with the same faculties as I have endowed thee, and have not driven him out of this world; couldst thou not have endured with him till he should have refreshed his hungry palate and rested his weary limbs?" And Abraham learned the attributes of God and was never intolerant thereafter.

—Oral tradition.

THE PROFIT IN ACCEPTING ADVICE.

A certain king had among a multitude of slaves one favorite whom he considered wiser than the rest, and upon whom he therefore bestowed a special favor by giving him his liberty, on condition, however, that he must sail for some other land. Thus, one bright day, a pinnace was supplied with provisions and other necessaries, and the slave was set adrift.

At first the sea was calm, but some days expired and a storm arose, tossing the little boat hither and thither, carrying it on the billowy waves further and further into the bosom of the tempest, with bût God to guide it and protect its solitary passenger. It lasted long but finally ceased ; the sea again became calm, and the freedman now fervently prayed to God to lead his pinnace to some shore. His prayer was heard, for he soon espied land, and sailing toward it he saw a multitude standing on the shore to welcome his arrival. Soon he reached the shore and he was seized amid cheers and great enthusiasm ; he was carried into a palatial mansion, robed in royal garments and proclaimed governor of the island. He at first believed himself to be dreaming, but soon became conscious of the reality, and seeing the subjects standing in obeisance before him and the servants awaiting his orders, the wise slave first of all demanded some counsellors. Shortly some hoary-headed men of dignified appearance placed themselves at his command, and to his inquiries about the governorship replied:

"The law of our island is to make every year another governor, and he must be a total stranger and a poor man. After the year he gets deposed and sent away, as poor as he came. Thus you were made our governor for one year."

"Could you advise me," inquired the governor, "what to do to save me from such cruel end?"

"Ah! we see that thou art wise!" replied they. "Thou doest well in asking advice, and we can certainly save thee if thou wilt do as we advise thee. Now, lose no time whilst thou hast the power. The whole colony is at thy disposal and the colonists at thy service. Take, therefore, men and material, send them to a neighboring island, build there up a colony, and when the time expires here let men from the other dominion await thee and carry thee thither where they shall serve thee forever."

The king is God, the wise slave the soul, the pinnace the human body, and life is the sea. The soul thus is placed into the pinnace, the body, supplied with provisions consisting of knowledge and understanding, and set afloat on life's tempestuous sea, which may be calm and smooth at first, but then the storms of life—conflict, struggle, and strife —will toss him hither and thither, and he finally accumulates enough to live in affluence. That is

his governorship, over which somebody else was
governor before, and somebody else will be again
after him.   He dies and he is sent off naked as he
came.   If he would but take advice he would provide for his future dominion by discreetly using
his wealth in doing good; and though he'll die
away from the terrestrial colony, his subjects*
from the celestial domains will be waiting for him,
to convey him to that dominion where they shall
ever and eternally serve him.

Chulin, 60 a.

---

* Tradition has it that every good deed or word creates a good
angel, and every bad or evil word an evil angel for the author : and
these angels receive the soul when it returns to its giver.   The evil
angels indict it and the good ones defend it.

BITTERER THAN DEATH.

At the time when Solomon, the Wise, had completed his book of "Ecclesiastes," the angel of death appeared before God, complaining that the wisest man on earth committed such a blunder as to write: "I find more bitter than death the woman whose heart is snares and nets" (Eccl. vii. 26). "What," said he, "knoweth a man of the bitterness of death? Can he express the feelings of a dying father leaving behind an affectionate wife and fond children, often in destitute condition? Or the pangs of a darling child dying among sobs and tears in the arms of loving parents? And many others who feel the deepest pangs that death can prepare?"

"What knowest thou," answered God, "of the bitterness a vicious woman administers? Suppose I grant thee but twenty years to live on earth, like other men, to search into this matter, that thou mayest then form thy opinion?"

The angel of death was willing, and leaving a substitute to fill his office, he soon was on earth in mortal shape, endowed with human proneness and frailties. He was not very long on earth ere he fell in love with a fair damsel who reciprocated the pleasure, and he proposed, she accepted, the marriage was consummated, and the angel of death was the happiest being on earth. But, ah! this felicity was not destined to be of long duration, for soon the wife began to be discontented with the ordinary mode of life, and desired fineries in superfluity, which her husband could not supply, and strife took the place of domestic bliss. It went from bad to worse, and the angel of death wished himself in heaven again, but he had to endure twenty years.

Oh, how sadly glided these years by! How many bitter, yes, exceedingly bitter doses had the angel of death to swallow ere he could leave his terrestrial abode! At last it came that he had to return to the celestial quarters, and as his conjugal life was blessed with a son, he now took him aside to give him a last parental admonition and a fond farewell.

He addressed him thus:

" My son, know now who I am—I am the angel of death, sent down to live here twenty years. My time is just now expiring, and I have to ascend to heaven again and leave thee here. I wish to provide for thee ere I go, and cannot do better than to advise thee to become a physician. Thou needest no other knowledge for that than thou possessest now; simply observe, when thou enterest the sick-room, whether I am there and where I will be standing; if I should not be there, or I should stand at the feet of the patient, anything thou wilt prescribe—say sugar water—will effect a cure. Shouldst thou, however, see me standing at the head of the patient, make no attempt to cure, for it will be of no avail, the patient must die;" and the celestial parent vanished. Acting on the instruction of his father, the son very wisely removed to where he was not known, and began the practice of medicine with marked success.

One day, it so happened that the magistrate of the city where the new doctor resided contracted a severe illness, and the most skilful physicians were summoned, but all were united in the opinion that there was no hope, and the new doctor was called in. As he entered the sick-chamber, alas! he, too, saw that there was no help. His father stood at the head of the patient. Determined to win fame, the new doctor gave orders to turn around the bed, so that, where the head was, the feet came to be, and the experiment proved successful. The angel of death now stood at the feet, and, true to his promise to his son, he had to spare the magistrate's life.

Soon thereafter, the king was seriously ill, and after all physicians had given him up, it was proposed to send for the new doctor, which they did, and he came. But, horror! This time the angel of death clung to the head of the king.

The new physician paced the floor up and down in deep meditation, and ordered all present to vacate the chamber, which was done. The doctor stood now pondering, and the angel of death, in faint expression, spoke:

"Give it up, my son; thou canst not outdo me this time."

"Well," replied the son, "I just wait for mama to

come, and I will consult her. She must be here
soon."

Away flew the father, muttering as he ran:

"Oh, if she is coming, I cannot stay! Her presence embittered my existence enough." And the
king was cured.

The angel of death was now brought before the
grand tribunal to answer why he neglected now
the second time to bring the required soul; and he
related his sad experience of the bitterness which is
bitterer than death, acknowledging that Solomon
was indeed wise. A vicious woman is more bitter
than death!

—Oral tradition.

PRIMEVAL MONOTHEISM.

Tradition has it that Abraham was cast into a burning furnace, and was not consumed nor scorched, while his brother Haran perished in the flames. It was then that holy-writ chronicled his death (Gen. xi. 28), and that Abraham was taken away from Ur by Terah, the father.

The inference is taken from the following passage: "Thou art the Lord, the God, who didst choose Abram, and broughtest him forth out of Ur of the Chaldees, and gavest him the name of Abraham."—Nehem. ix. 7. It translates Ur flame or fire (as in Isaiah, xliv. 16; Ezek., v. 2), hence Abraham was brought forth, not out of Ur, but out of the fire prepared for his cremation in Chaldees. The cause of it was his resistance to worship the fire, and the legend runs thus:

Terah,* the father of Abraham, was a manufacturer of idols of every description. He worshipped them, and furnished others with their respective gods. One day business took him away from home, and he left Abraham in charge of the business at home.

Soon a purchaser came, and Abraham asked him, "How old are you?" "So and so many

---

* It is supposed that idols took the name terafim in Hebrew from Terah, the manufacturer of idols.

-years," was the reply. "How can a man of your age bow down before and worship an image that is scarcely a day old?" queried Abraham; and the purchaser departed, ashamed and enlightened. And so Abraham enlightened every customer that came, until there came an old woman with a dish of fine flour, requesting him to offer it up to the gods. In great displeasure, Abraham took a rod and broke all the images into shatters, sparing the largest one, into whose hands he affixed the rod. As the father came home, he saw the devastation, and asked Abraham how this happened, to which Abraham replied: "Father, why should I hide the fact? There came an old woman with a dish of fine flour as an offering to the gods, and as I placed it before them, each wanted to be first at eating, and they became so disorderly that the biggest took the rod, and shattered them all to pieces."

"Why, boy! dost thou dare to mock me?" cried Terah, angrily. "How can they move? They have no life!"

"Why, father," retorted Abraham, "do thy ears not hear what thy mouth speaketh? They cannot move; they have no life, yet are gods, objects of worship and adoration!"

For this offense Terah took his son before the mighty Nimrod that he might punish or admonish him, and Nimrod commanded the iconoclast to worship the fire.

"Why not rather the water?" said Abraham. "Is not water mightier than fire? It extinguishes it."

"Be it then so," replied Nimrod, "worship the water."

"Why not the clouds?" asked Abraham further; "do not the clouds carry the water?"

"So let it be the clouds," replied Nimrod.

"Why not the winds?" protested Abraham; "do not the winds disperse the clouds?"

"So let it be the winds," yielded Nimrod.

"Let us then worship man," retorted Abraham. "Man is mightier than the winds; he can build them out of his dwellings."

"Boy, darest thou mock me!" exclaimed Nimrod, discomposed. "I worship the fire, and now I will see whether thy God will save thee from my god." And a big fire was made, into which Abraham was cast. Haran, his brother, witnessing all this, thought, if Abraham will be saved, I will join him; if not, I remain with Nimrod. Abraham came forth alive and unhurt before all eyes. Now Haran was asked what god he believed in, and he said in Abraham's God, for which offence he, too, was cast into the burning flames, but he was consumed. Then Terah took his son Abraham, and Lot, the son of Haran, and moved from Ur to Canaan.

WHO IS ADMITTED TO HEAVEN.

Once upon a time there died a man of great religious zeal, and as he appeared at heaven's gate, he boldly knocked, calling aloud: "Open, open the gates wherein the righteous enter, that I may come in!" "Who art thou?" called a voice in return. "I am a devout Catholic," replied the applicant. "Catholic! Catholic!" sounded the voice of the gate-keeper in accents of amazement; "we know of no Catholics here, and thou canst not come in." Like a thunderbolt struck these words upon the ear of the disappointed religionist. "Is this indeed possible?" murmured he to himself. "Is it possible that I would not be admitted to heaven, having lived all my lifetime in piety and religiousness? Never did I eat any meat on Fridays; I went regularly to mass and confession, and should I now be, instead of rewarded, debarred from the celestial kingdom?" As he thus meditated, there came another individual to seek admittance to heaven, and seeing the Catholic standing before the gate muttering to himself, asked him what was the matter, and received the reply: "I was an ardent Catholic all my lifetime, and now I am refused admittance to heaven." "Oh, well," declared the new comer, "I knew all my lifetime that Catholics cannot go to heaven. I am a Protestant. Now wait and see how promptly I will be admitted," and he knocked at the gate. "Who's there?" sounded a shrill voice. "I, so and so, a zealous Protestant!" was the confident reply. "A Protestant! What creature is that?" inquired the gate keeper. "We have no Protestants here, nor know I what it means. Thou canst not enter these portals." And the poor Protestant, shocked and disheartened, remained also standing outside at heaven's gate. It was not long before a sullen Moslem came on the same errand, and the two Christians, knowing his religion by his garb, asked him curiously: "Dost thou really expect to be admitted to heaven? Why, see us; we are Christians, and yet could not enter, how shouldst thou enjoy that blessed privilege?" "Ah," said the Mussulman, "Allah will take me to his bosom when he would not turn to a Christian," and he, too, knocked at the gate. "Who's there?" came the voice, as before, to the others. "A meek disciple of Mohammed's creed," answered the son of the Orient. "We know here of no such name, and thou canst not gain admission under such an appellative," was the gate-keeper's reply, and he, too, was left standing outside. Scarcely had the three exchanged a few words regarding their unfortunate position, when another one approached, having a long gray beard, and his visage and nose at once stamped him as a Jew. When he had heard that the Christians and the Mohammedan were refused admittance, he thought that he, being of God's chosen people, would be unhesitatingly ushered into the kingdom of heaven; and he knocked at the gate as did the others before him. "Who's there?" resounded again the voice; to which the Jew reliantly replied: "A Yehudi." The gate keeper impatiently replied: "What sects are those troubling me these four times— Catholics, Protestants, Mohammedans, and Jews! We have no such sects here, and thou canst not gain admission," and the poor son of Abraham, too, was left to join the three disappointed applicants for heavenly admittance.

Meanwhile the bells underneath them on the terrestrial hemisphere began to toll, calling the attention of the pilgrims to the approach of night, reminding them of the worship of God, ere Somnus descends to the sons of earth; and the Catholic threw himself on his knees, the Protestant bowed in reverence, the Mussulman prostrated himself, and the Jew turned toward the east, each praying in his mode and custom.

The sacred devotion over, the Jew addressed his three companions thus: "It seems there is a mistake somewhere, and from all appearances we are doomed to stay this night here. What the coming day may bring forth, none can foretell. To pray, each has his ritual and peculiar custom, but I have a little volume with me which I call Scriptures (you call it Old Testament), but we all concur in its contents; let us read it together, and pass the time with religious devotion." All joined in reading, and (as it happened) they read the second chapter and tenth verse of Malachi:

" Have we not all One Father? Hath not one God created us?" when suddenly the gate above them opened, and the gate keeper called to them: "Why did ye not say so before, and ye would have been admitted? As the children of one God and one common Father, all find abode in this vast eternal domain, but by no appellations are they known here."

—Original.

THE SERPENT.

" And the Lord said unto him, What is that in thine hand? And he said, A rod.

And he said, Cast it on the ground. And he cast it on the ground, and it became a serpent; and Moses fled from before it.

And the Lord said unto Moses, Put forth thine hand, and take it by the tail. And he put forth his hand, and caught it, and it became a rod in his hand."—*Exod.* iv. 2-4.

As Adam was expelled from the garden of Eden he took with him a bough from that tree that bore the fruit which caused his doom, for an everlasting remembrance. This he shaped afterwards into a rod (or staff) and engraved on it the ineffable name of " *Ellohim.*" This staff became a family relic, passing through generations from Adam to Noah, from Noah to Abraham, Isaac, and Jacob (who speaks of this staff in Gen. xxxii. 12), who, as a matter of course, brought it to Egypt into the house of his son Joseph; and when the Israelites were enslaved by the Egyptians after the death of Joseph, everything belonging to the house of Jacob and Joseph fell into the possession of Pharaoh. This staff remained there also.

Jethro, so says tradition, was formerly a court official in Egypt, but he had committed a treasonable offence and to escape punishment he fled from Egypt to Midian, where he afterwards became a priest. He took nothing with him in his haste of flight but this relic of Adamic origin —the staff—and wonderfully enough he was fortunate in his flight.

Some years afterwards when Moses fled from Egypt, he settled down (Scriptures relate) in Jethro's house, and for forty years nothing remarkable transpired with him. One day Moses noticed, for the first time, in Jethro's garden a staff with the name of God wonderfully engraved on it, he grasped it with joy and went with it to his usual avocation. That day the Lord appeared to him in the burning bush, and among other signs the Lord told him to cast away the rod, which when Moses did so turned into a serpent. Moses became frightened and wanted to retreat, but the Lord told him not to fear, but to take hold of it; and when Moses did so the serpent became a rod again.

This rod—or staff—is the name of God, and the Lord gave Moses the sign for practical illustration: Cast away the name of God and it will invariably turn into a serpent apt to destroy your *paradise*—your bliss and happiness. Should it, however, so happen that you did cast from you the rod—the name of God—or otherwise fell from your hand, and it turned into a serpent, fear not! It is not too late to take hold of it. Face the serpent and grasp her in your hand! and she will surely turn into a defensive rod again, *i. e.* God will be your defense again.

—Jashar—Exod.

A TIME FOR RELIGION.

" Let thy garments be white at all times."

Eccl. ix. 8.

A monarch once had assembled such of his subjects as he loved best, and presented them each with
a suit of clothes, as a token of esteem. Some of
them had prized this gift so highly that they laid
them carefully into a chest and wore them only
at special occasions, thus preserving them to
be always neat and clean. Others, however, have
taken less care of them; while still others wore
them daily, performing in them the most menial
labor. One day the subjects were again called
before the monarch and ordered to appear in these
garments. Those priding themselves with the
gift appeared attired neat and clean, just as on
the day they were received. The others had their
clothes stained and well worn out; but the third
party appeared torn and ragged. " How is this? "
asked the monarch, " why have these men preserved their garments in such good condition and clean,
while you have so bestained them and the others
have them all in rags and tatters ? " " We," said
the first party, " have only worn them on special
occasions, when we could manifest that it was

honorable to wear them; at other times they were stored away in a chest."

"We," said the other party, "thought fit to remember the king oftener than at mere special occasions, and wore his gift more."

"And we," said the third party, "wanted to have the king ever before us; thinking that in all our avocations of life, in our labors as well as in our pleasures, his garments should be worn." "Yes," said the monarch, "but you cannot sit in my parlor; you are unfit to be received in a king's palace;" and they had to withdraw in shame and disdain, but the first party remained and spent a pleasurable time with the monarch.

This monarch is the Holy One, blessed be He; the subjects he loved best is Israel,* and the garments he gave them is His holy religion. Some deem it a high prize, and consider it an honor to possess this religion and are religious at proper times, i. e., in the synagogues, in the houses of worship, or at ceremonials; all other times they have religion stored away in a chest—their inner-most recesses. They move in every society and circle as men with proper respect. There are, however, some who with their fanatic ways bestain true religion; while still others disgrace religion. In every corner they strew their religion; in the streets they talk religion; and detest those that do not agree with their religious views, so that

---

* Israel was chosen by God as His standard-bearers, because they were first to recognize the true God, and the rabbins had that in view when they wrote their legends and allegories of this kind.

their religion becomes at last like that garment bestained, bespotted, and fragmented. God will surely not regard their observances, for they are irreligious, and unfit them for the godly habitation; the former, however, that have been an honor to mankind and useful to the world will undoubtedly be regarded by God worthy of inhabiting the royal palaces of the celestial abode. This it was that Solomon had in view when he said: "Let thy garments be white at all times."

Sabbath, cix.

EVIDENCE FROM NATURE.

A rich merchant, once travelling over land and sea with rich wares, arrived at Sura (in Egypt), where he fell sick, becoming unconscious before he could make his will, and died.

He had with him a servant, who now proclaimed himself his son, and with none to doubt it became the possessor of the deceased merchant's fortune. With this wealth he soon rose to eminence, that introduced him into the highest rank of society, and it became him easy to connect himself in marriage with families of renown, and become influential himself.

The wife of the above merchant, with an infant child, a boy, waited long for intelligence from her husband, but it came in vain.

She began to be uneasy and made inquiries, but the distance where he died was so great, that it took a long time ere she could obtain the slightest clue of his demise, and when she was informed of her husband's death, she knew not what to do, and bore the misfortune patiently without making any further steps.

Years have gone by, and the child became a young man able to hold his position, and he determined to go in quest of his father's grave and inheritance.

The distance was long, but Sura was reached, and he soon learned with the greatest certainty that his father died there, and that his servant assumed the place of a son, enjoying now his wealth. What could he, a stranger, do when the servant was now of high standing and a citizen? He visited the Rabbi Saadja, and laid before him his grievance. The rabbi advised him to go to the king, and lay the matter before him, which he did. The king summoned the accused, but he firmly and emphatically denounced the claimant as an impostor, claiming himself to be the son and rightful heir. Rabbi Saadja, who stood high in court, was called and his counsel solicited. He meditated a while, then contrived an original plan. He advised that the grave be opened, and a small bone from the deceased be brought. That done, he ordered some blood to be drawn from both claimants into two separate vessels, and the bone was dipped first into the blood of the servant, but the bone was not affected in the least; the bone was then dipped into the blood of the lately arrived son, and the bone became saturated, drawing into itself the blood. This was taken as clear evidence, and the deceiver had to yield his fortune to the rightful heir.

—*Simchath hannefesh*, xii. 12.

WISE MOURNING.

Rabbi Meier* had two sons that were his pride and his jewels; and as one Sabbath the sage tarried a while in the synagogue, these two children were suddenly seized by the cruel grip of death, and both lay lifeless in one hour. The shrieks and cries of the tender mother could not restore them to life; she had therefore resolved not to destroy the Sabbathic peace and happiness of her affectionate husband; nor frighten him with the sudden calamitous news, and she laid the two boys side by side on their couch, closing their dear eyes and covering them up.

Rabbi Meier returned from the house of God, with happiness pictured on his countenance, and asked for his children to bless them,† but Beruriah,‡ the affectionate wife and fond mother, sweetly replied: " They went to the house of God and are doubtless tarrying on their way; come, dear husband, eat your meal, the Lord is with them and they may soon return." The invitation was so cordial and sweet, that the rabbi could not

---

* A disciple of Akiba.

† It is customary with Jews to bless their children when returning from divine services.

‡ Daughter of Hanina ben Theradion.

detect her sorrow, and performing his *habdalah* service (a ceremony which concludes the Sabbath), he partook with his loving and beloved wife of a dainty meal, after which Beruriah began: " Rabbi, pray let me ask thy advice. A friend gave me some time ago a very valuable jewel that I shall keep it safely for him, and being in my possession so long, I became attached to it, and would dislike to part with it ; but here comes my friend, and asks me for the jewels, what shall I do ? "

" Why, Beruriah, my beloved wife! Canst thou ask me a question like this? Shouldst thou have a thing that is not thine?" retorted R. Meier. " Thou shalt, of course, return it." " Come then, dear husband," said Beruriah, " and let me show thee that jewel," and she led him to the bedside where lay in deep slumber their two darlings, like two flowers nipped in the bud. As she uncovered them the father began to lament, but the mother reproached him, " What, O Rabbi ! Wouldst thou keep a thing that is not thine? God gave them to us, and now He demands them back," and both lifted their eyes heavenward, repeating the words solemnly and sincerely : " The Lord hath given and the Lord hath taken away, and the name of the Lord be praised !"

—*Midr. Jalkut*, iii. 165.

CONTENTMENT.

There lived once a man good and pious, who in his absolute confidence in God accepted everything, the good and the evil, alike; as he used to say, " Whatever God doeth is to our good." *

He once went on a journey, and took with him a donkey to ride on, a torch for light on dark nights, and a cock to announce time—as in those days there were no watches, clocks, or any mechanical time keepers. On his journey he arrived in a town late in the day, and wished to tarry there over night, but he was unable to procure lodging ; although he went from house to house, and offered to pay for his shelter. The weary traveller continued his journey without a murmur, expressing his favorite maxim, " What God doeth is for the best." He rode on till he reached a forest, and too tired to go further, he halted beneath a heavily shaded tree, lighted his torch, fastened his donkey, and offering up a prayer to God commending his spirit into His care, he laid himself down to sleep. But scarcely had he closed his eyes, when

---

* This is ascribed to Akiba by some; others again state that it was Nahum the Gam Zoo, who used to say to every misfortune that befell him, Gam Zoo l'toba " (this is also for the best), which maxim is still extant with pious and God fearing Jews.

the roaring of a lion awoke him, who, in the next moment, devoured his donkey. Happy over the thought that the lion did not attack him, he muttered, "Indeed, what God doeth is for our best." In another instant a marten sped by, grasping the cock and ran away with it; and before the poor solitary traveller could reflect on it, a storm arose and suddenly extinguished his torch, leaving him in the dark, and alone in the endless forest.

The coming morning he learned from other travellers that the village which refused him shelter was visited by robbers, who pillaged many houses and killed many people.

"Whence came these robbers?" asked the pious traveller astonished. "They came from this very direction," said they, "and we really wonder that thou hast escaped them." "Ah, I see now!" exclaimed the pious traveller, raising his eyes heavenward. "What God doeth is for our best!' How if the donkey would have brayed, or the cock crowed! or how if the light of the torch would have attracted the attention of these robbers! They would have destroyed me. Indeed, 'what God doeth is for the best!'"

—*Berachoth*, ix.

SELF-DEPENDENCE.

Eliezer ben Dordeja was a man leading a reckless life, and one day, as he was listening to a woman for whom he had high regards, he was seriously affected by her remark, " Eliezer, the son of Dordeja, will hardly ever become repentant." With a look of despair he repaired to the hills, and, seating himself between the rocks at the mountains he prayed aloud, " O rock and mountains, pray ye to God for me that He may have mercy on me!" but they echoed in response, " Ere we pray for thee we must pray for ourselves; for holy-writ says that ' The mountains shall depart and the hills be removed.' "—(Isaiah liv. 10.)

He then looked up to the heavens and then cast his eyes to the earth as he implored them, " O ye heavens and earth! pray ye for me to God for mercy!" and they replied, " Ere we pray for thee we must pray for ourselves; for holy-writ has it that ' The heavens shall vanish like smoke, and the earth wax old like a garment.' "—(Isaiah li. 6.)

" Oh, then, pray ye for me, ye sun and moon!" pleaded he; but sun and moon replied, " Ere we pray for thee we must pray for ourselves; for is it not written in holy-writ, " The moon shall be confounded and the sun be ashamed?'"—(Isaiah xxiv. 23.)

"Oh, then, pray ye for me, ye stars and planets!" cried he most piteously; but they replied, "Ere we pray for thee we must pray for ourselves; for is it not written in holy-writ, 'And all the hosts of heaven shall be dissolved?'"—(Isaiah xxxiv. 4.)

"Ah, then!" moaned he, "then all depends upon myself!" and he drooped his sorrowing head between his knees amidst sighing and sobbing until his spirit departed. There came then a voice from heaven proclaiming: "Rabbi Eliezer ben Dordeja has repented and inherited the portion of the future world!"

From this we infer that all, from the smallest to the greatest, have enough to do for themselves; and we must not ask others to do for us what we can do ourselves, even in praying.

—*Aboda Zorah f.*, lxxi. 1.

DUE REWARD.

Emperor Adrian, in passing once a street in Tiberias, noticed an old man planting a tree, and he stepped nearer and asked him, " Why plantest thou that tree, an old man as thou art? Couldst thou not have worked in thy early youth enough for thy old age? Thou canst surely eat no more fruit of this tree?" " I have worked in my youth even as I work now," replied the old man, "and if it is God's will I may yet enjoy the fruit of this tree."

"How old art thou?" asked the emperor. " I am a hundred years old," replied the old man. " A hundred years, and still expect to enjoy the fruit of his tree!" exclaimed Adrian in astonishment. " If it is God's will," replied the old man complacently; "and if not, I will leave it for my son as my father had left some fruit trees for me to enjoy." The emperor Adrian was by no means well disposed towards Jews, but the spirit of this old man so pleased him that before he took leave he told him who he was, and, " shouldst thou live till this tree bear fruit, I wish you to come and see me." The tree grew up to bear fruit, and the old man yet lived hearty and hale. He remembered Adrian's request, and he filled a basket with figs of that tree and carried it to the royal palace.

Admitted into the emperor's presence, he was at once recognized and received very cordially. The basket was emptied of the fruit it contained and filled up with gold. Thus the old man departed rewarded, jubilant and delighted

The courtiers, after he was gone, could refrain no longer, and asked the emperor, " How comes it that a monarch like thee should so honor a Jew as thou has just honored this old man?" "Should I not honor a man," replied the emperor, " whom the Lord has honored, of which his old age is proof?"

A neighbor of this old man had a very selfish wife, and hearing of this old man's success at court, imagined that the emperor was fond of figs, and urged her husband to load up a big basket with choice figs and take it to him, thinking of getting plenty of gold for it. Arrived at the imperial palace, he related to the guard that he had learned of the emperor's great love for figs, and that he had brought a big basket full of it, hoping to obtain a good reward. The emperor was apprised of this, and guessing the right reason of this man's gift, ordered him to stand in the hallway of the palace, and caused him to be pelted with his own figs. Sore and besmeared, he returned to his disappointed wife, and told her of his unfortunate adventure. But she could only console him with the words, " Be thou content that they were not citrons, or else thou wouldst have fared far worse."

—Rabboth, 193 *b.*

WOMAN'S CONSTANCY.

There lived in Sidon a husband and wife who loved each other tenderly, but ten years' wedlock found them yet childless, which the husband took much to heart, and, God-fearing as he was, he visited the rabbi, Simon bar Jochai,* laying before him the matter and asked for a divorce.† To his wife he tenderly said, "Return, beloved, to thy father's house and live in God and peace there, for we are childless. To give thee evidence of my love and esteem, I permit thee to take from my house whatsoever thou appreciatest best." The rabbi, hearing this, advised them, "You were wedded with a feast and why not part with a feast? Let the world know that there is no reproach in either of you, and that it is only childlessness that causes you to part;" which advice was well taken, and they readily agreed to make a feast like that of a wedding. The affectionate wife preparing dainties in abundance, and at the feast she administered to her husband, extending to him wine, cup after cup, which he could not

---

* Lived at the close of the second century.

† Rashi on the commentary of Genesis xvi. 3 speaks of a custom that prevailed some time, that a childless wedlock, after ten years, was sufficient ground for divorce. According to tradition it was considered a disfavor of God, and a divorce was granted.

refuse, thinking this to be the last meal together; and he became so intoxicated that he knew not what was going on around him. Now the loving wife summoned some faithful servants who with tenderness carried the husband into her father's house, laying him upon a soft couch, where he slept while she kept watch over him. During the night he awoke, and, seeing he was not in his house, asked, "Where am I?" "You are in my father's house, my dearest, and that according to your own words," was the sweet reply of the wife. "You have told me to go to my father's house, and take from your house that which I appreciate best. Nothing could I find in your house that I love and appreciate more than you, and I have brought you therefore to my father's house." He could utter no words at hearing such confession from the lips of one he really loved, and he but stretched out his arm and clasped her to his heart, and his thoughts wandered up to God in gratefulness that He, after all, decreed that he should have such a faithful, pious and affectionate wife. It is needless to say that the divorce was not asked nor given, and the rabbi's plan worked well. The Lord also looked down upon them in mercy, for in another year their union was blessed with a male child.

—*Jalkut,* v. a.

HANDSOME IS WHO HANDSOME DOES.

Joshua ben Chananiah was greatly esteemed by the court of Rome on account of his unlimited wisdom and learning, but his personal appearance was very uncomely. One day he happened to be at the royal palace, and the princess, after hearing his wisdom, exclaimed, "Oh, what a homely receptacle for such wisdom!" Joshua, composed, and without evincing the least sign of having been offended, entered into conversation with the princess, and directing his subject towards affairs so that he had the opportunity to ask where the emperor kept his wines, the princess informed him that their wines were kept in earthen vessels. "Why!" exclaimed the Hebrew, "I am astonished that you keep such good wine as the emperor drinks in an earthen vessel, why not in gold or silver vessels?" "Methinks thou art right," responded the princess ; and no sooner had Joshua left, than she ordered all the best wines to be emptied and filled into gold and silver caskets. In a short time thereafter the emperor perceived that his beverages began to get sour, and, on inquiry, he learned what the daughter had done. He at once sent for her, and she explained that it was Joshua who advised it. Joshua was sent for, and he disclaimed that he advised it, "but," said he, " the princess wondered at my wisdom being encased in such homely vessel as my appearance is, and I asked why the wines of the emperor should be kept in earthen and not in gold and sil ver vessels ; if she would have understood what I was aiming at, the lesson would have been completed then ; as it is, however, she can now see it practically. Wisdom is seldom connected with beauty, for the temptations the prepossessing appearance offers are meant to irritate wisdom, besides the vanity it imparts."

—Taanith, 7 a.

THE MEASURE YOU MEASURE WITH IS MEASURED UNTO YOU.

In the "Ethics of Our Forefathers" (Pirke Aboth, i. 7) there is a maxim laid down by Joshua ben Perachia to judge everybody favorably. A certain man was once hired to work for an agreed salary, and worked for three years without having drawn the same. He desired to go home and demanded his accumulations from his employer, but he very piteously said, "I really have just now no money." "Give me then some of your produce," demanded the employé. "I regret very much," said the master, "that I cannot comply with this, thy term." He asked him for cattle, for wine or vineyard, but the master declared he was unable to give him anything. With a heavy sigh the poor laborer took his tools without a murmur and departed. Scarcely had he gone when the employer took the money he owed him, and had three asses laden with eatables, with drinkables, and with wearing apparel, and rode after him. Arrived at the house of the laborer a meal was prepared, and they ate and drank together; after which the employer drew forth the money and handed it to the employé, and ordered his servants to unload the asses also. The following dialogue then ensued:

Employer. " What didst thou think when I told thee that I had no money ? "

Employé. " I thought that thou hast unfortunately lost it."

Employer. " What hast thou thought when I told thee that I had no cattle ? "

Employé.   " I thought that thou mightest have owed it to others previous to my debt."

Employer. " What hast thou thought when I told thee I had no field ? "

Employé. " I thought that it might have been mortgaged."

Employer. " What hast thou thought when I told thee I had no fruit ? "

Employé. " I thought that it might not have been tithed yet."

Employer. " What hast thou thought when I told thee I had no vineyard nor wine ? "

Employé. " I thought thou mightest have sanctified it to the service of God."

Employer. " Ah, thou art a godly man ! Faithfully hast thou complied with the ethical doctrine 'Judge everybody favorably.'   Thou hast judged me favorably and may God judge thee favorably."

—*Sab.*, 127.

THE WICKEDNESS OF SODOM.

" And the Lord said, the cry of Sodom and
Gomorrah is indeed great, and their sin is very
grievous."—Genesis xviii. 20.

Among the heinous outrages committed by the
Sodomites a few are noteworthy to relate : It was
customary that every one should give a coin to a
mendicant, but when he was to purchase bread or
any food the coin was not accepted in pay, and
often the unfortunate victim had to starve.

As to hospitality, there was an inn for strangers
with a rather small bed in it, into which they laid
the visitor, and if he was shorter than the bed, the
wicked Sodomites stretched him till he was long
enough for the bed ; and if he was taller, they cut
his legs off to suit the size.

It once so happened that Eliezer, the servant of
Abraham, visited Sodom, and all were officious to
conduct him to the infamous inn and were urgent
that he should lie in the bed, but the faithful
servant of the Hebrew patriarch suspected something wrong, declared that he vowed never to
sleep in a bed, and he slept on the floor, thus
escaped the terrible torture. As one day he walked
in the street one of the citizens attacked and struck
him so that the blood dripped from the wound.
Eliezer sought a judge and laid the matter before

him. "What!" said the judge, "hast thou yet cause to complain when one of our citizens bleeds you free of charge?" and fined him to the amount that bleeding would cost by a surgeon. At this sentence Eliezer fell upon the judge dealing him a heavy blow, so that the judge was bleeding. "How darest thou!" cried the judge. "How dare I," retorted Eliezer. "I only bled thee free of charge. Now pay the fine thyself to the one who bled me." As Eliezer was not punished, he was doubtless considered worthy of the association of the Sodomites.

—*Sanhedrin*, 109 *b*.

MARTYRDOM OF HANINA.

It was about sixty years after the destruction of the second temple at Jerusalem, under the reign of Adrian (or Hadrian), that the Jews suffered terrible and severe persecution; and only because they would not renounce their faith and accept that of the Roman's persuasion. Every observance of the Mosaic or Rabbinic code was interdicted, and even the reading of the Scriptures was forbidden. Woe was unto him who was discovered reading them! Often was it punished with death. This, however, made Israel cling together more closely; it made them more dutiful to their religious observances, more faithful to the creed their ancestors confessed to, and more firm in their belief for which they sacrificed their comfort and often their lives. The persecution was especially severe on the rabbis and teachers.

Hanina ben Theradion was discovered reading a scroll * containing the holy-writ, and he was seized and brought before the tribunal, where he was mercilessly sentenced to death on the stake. They have heaped around him sheaves of rice straw and set on fire, and, in order that he should not expire too quick, a saturated sponge was laid on his chest which was kept moist. The daughter, on beholding this, shrieked aloud, "O father, must I see thee suffer thus!" "My daughter," replied Hanina in his agony, "were I to be burned alone

---

* Scriptures in those days were all written on parchment scrolls.

it would be very hard, but the scroll of my faith is burned along with me; and He who will visit the ignominy of the law of God will also visit my ignominy."

His disciples, hearing this, inquired, " O Rabbi, tell us what thou seest?" "Ah, my sons," responded the nearly expiring martyr, " I see the parchment consumed by the fire, but the letters ascend unhurt." *   Seeing him suffer terrible agony, they called to him, " Why, O Master, not open thy mouth, inhale the flames that thy suffering may end and let thy pure soul ascend on high?" " It is better," replied the sage, "that He who gave it shall take it again than I should hasten to take my life." †

The executioner, hearing all this, addressed the martyr, " O master, if I should remove the sponge and increase the flames, thus shortening thy agony, wilt thou supplicate that I may inherit the kingdom of heaven?" " I will," said Hanina. " Then swear to me," was the torturer's demand; and the martyr swore.   The sponge was removed and the fire stirred, and the soul of Hanina ben Theradion took instantly its flight.   At this instant the Roman too cast himself into the flames, and a voice was heard to call, " Hanina ben Theradion and his executioner inherited the kingdom of heaven."

—*Berachoth*, 9.

---

* Meaning that all books of Scriptures may be destroyed, yet its spirit never.

† Here a lesson is conveyed, whatever trouble, sorrow or the severest tribulation visits us, we must never take our lives. Let Him who gave it take it.

Akiba, like Hanina, would also not abandon the reading and studying of the law of God; he, moreover, went around teaching his brethren and urging them to be steadfast and trust in God.

Papus ben Jehudah was astonished at this and asked him, "O master, fearest thou not the tyrant's mandate?" But Akiba promptly rebuked him: "Papus, whom people call wise, art thou such a coward? Let this parable teach thee: A fox passing along the shore of a river noticed the fishes excitedly swimming hither and thither, as they were in terror and fear, and he asked them why they were so terrified and excited. 'Why, indeed,' said the poor inhabitants of the water, 'seest thou not the nets that are spread out to entrap us?' 'Come then,' said the sly fox, 'unto the land and dwell here in safety.' 'Ah, indeed!' said the fishes, 'art thou the fox, the wise among beasts? If danger threatens us here where we are accustomed to live, how much more will it threaten us where our death is sure?' Thus, O Papus, can we say. If we should fear the danger when we do observe the laws of God, how much more have we to fear if we abandon them?"

Shortly thereafter Rabbi Akiba was seized and cast into prison for reading God's law; and not

long thereafter Papus incurred the displeasure of
the Roman court and was also cast into prison.

Here the two met again; but Papus ruefully
expressed his bitter regret, "Akiba, Akiba! thou
sufferest as a martyr; but I, alas, have violated
God's law to be in favor with the Romans, and
yet my prospects are as bad as yours, besides I
suffer as a criminal."

Akiba then, like Hanina, was burned at the stake,
and amidst his agonizing pain his disciples moaned
and cried, "O rabbi, rabbi, how must thou
suffer!" "Yes!" said Akiba woefully, "but all
my lifetime I have been teaching the sublime pre-
cept, 'Thou shalt love the Lord thy God with all
thy heart, with all thy soul and with all thy might,'
should I now not lay down my life willingly for
this noble work? Yes, my life I gladly sacrifice
for God's holy law. *Sh'ma Israel adonoy ellohainoo,
adonoy echod!* (Hear, O Israel, the Eternal is our
God, the Eternal is one! *) at the last word his
soul took flight, and a voice was heard to call:
"Happy art thou, Akiba, who hast died while
Echod left thy lips! The future world shall be thy
inheritance."

— *Aboda Zarah,* 18.

---

* This passage is embodied in every prayer of Israelites, private
or public, and it said as the last words at one's dying bed.

NEVER TOO LATE TO LEARN.

Rabbi Akiba * at forty was void of all knowledge and only knew how to be a shepherd, in which capacity he was employed by a wealthy Jew at Jerusalem, named Kalba Shebua. There sprang up between him and his employer's daughter a mutual love, but, owing to his total ignorance, the maiden's parents opposed the alliance. Notwithstanding this opposition, however, the lovers were united in wedlock, and when the father heard of it he disowned his daughter, and Akiba and his wife lived in great want and destitution. If Akiba had but learned and become a scholar the parents-in-law would have gladly recognized him as son-in-law, but this was now a matter out of question, as he was too old to begin. One day he passed a spring where a stone seemed to be hollowed out by the water which constantly dripped on it, and it impressed him so that he began to reason with himself: Could a stone become so impressed by water, and why not a human heart by the words of God? He immediately bid good-by to his beloved and loving wife and repaired to Jamnia,†

---

* One of the ten martyrs in Israel. He died under the reign of Hadrian at the stake, as described in another part of this volume.

† A well populated seaport town at the time of the Maccabees, and a seat of great rabbinical learning.

where he entered the academy of R. Joshua and began to study hard and earnestly. He soon became an excellent scholar, and his great zeal and energy made him afterwards a renowned teacher and master, under whose tuition not less than twenty-four thousand pupils were graduated. When he returned to Jerusalem, it is useless to describe with what transport of joy his parents-in-law received him and embraced him as son-in-law.

Tradition agrees with history in giving him a lifetime of one hundred and twenty years.

Maimonides was also far advanced in years when he began to study. In his childhood's days he disliked schools, and his father one day severely upbraided him, and Moses (Maimonides) took it so to heart that he left home, sought admittance into a college and became afterward a great distinguished scholar.

—*Kethuboth*, 62—*Nedarim*, 50.

NO ESCAPE FROM PUNISHMENT.

How could the Lord impose punishment upon the sinner after he departed this world? Cannot the soul say, I am not at fault, it is the body that carried me to sinfulness, behold, since I left it I am sinless? and cannot the body say, I am but clay and since the soul has left me I am immovable, from which it becomes evident that without the soul I cannot sin. It is the soul, therefore, that prompted me to sin? Let the following allegory explain:

A prince, having had a desirable garden and wishing to have it guarded by such watchmen who cannot steal the fruit themselves, employed a blind and a lame man; the blind could hear the approach of intruders and give the alarm, or in case he should not hear, the lame will see and call aloud. The prince had one favorite tree bearing an excellent fruit, and the lame man one day described in such glowing manner the fruit to the blind confrère that he became desirous of eating it, and began to induce the lame comrade to go and pluck some of it. "How can we?" said the lame man, "I cannot climb and thou canst not see." "Easy enough," said the blind man. "I will stoop down and you stand on my shoulders. I will then arise and you will pluck the fruit;" and thus they robbed the tree of its luscious product. The prince, coming to inspect his garden, found his favorite fruit gone and called upon the watchmen to give account, but the blind one claimed he could not see and the lame one claimed he could not climb, hence they knew not who stole the fruit. The wise prince understood their scheme, and placed the lame man on the shoulders of the blind, and said, "this is the way ye have robbed my fruit, and this is the way I shall punish both of you."

Likewise will the omniscient God judge the body and the soul, both shall suffer, for both are guilty.

—*Rabboth*, 169 *b, and Jalkut*, 123 *a.*

GOD'S LAW IN QUALITY, NOT IN QUAN-TITY.

> " And ye shall observe my statutes and my judgments which man shall do and live in them."—Lev. xviii. 15.

From this we infer that the statutes and judgments of God were given for man to govern his moral life, and though it was necessary in Moses' time to expand them to six hundred and thirteen, David condensed them to eleven in his fifteenth Psalm : " O Lord, who shall sojourn in thy tent? Who shall dwell on thy holy mountain? He that is upright and acteth justly, and speaketh the truth with his heart ; having no slander on his tongue, nor doeth any evil to his neighbor, and beareth no reproach to him that come near him. The vile person is contemned in his eyes ; but honoreth those that fear the Lord, swearing away evil and changeth not his oath. His money he giveth not in usury, and takes no bribe against the innocent. He that doeth these shall never be moved."

Isaiah composes them into six in his thirty-third chapter, verse 15 :

" He that walketh righteously and speaketh uprightly, despising the gain of oppressions, shaking his hands from obtaining bribe ; who stoppeth his ears from hearing blood-guiltiness, and shutteth his eyes from beholding evil. He shall dwell on high," etc.

Micah incloses them in but three, Micah vi. 8:

" And what doth the Lord require of thee but to do justly, and to love mercy ; and walk humbly before the Lord thy God."

Later on Isaiah reproduced them, making but two, Isaiah lvi. 1:

" Observe ye justness and do rignteousness."

Amos in his 5th chapter, 4th verse, comprises them in but one :

" Thus sayeth the Lord to the house of Israel: Seek ye me and live." Our sages say, from this we can infer that in seeking God we comply with His law. Habakuk (chapter ii. 4) expresses gloriously : " The just shall live in his faith."

—*Maccoth*, 23 *b*.

THE YOUTHFUL COMFORTERS.

" And Haman was filled with anger."—Esther v. 9.

At the time when all Jews of Medo-Persia were wrapt in deep gloom and mourning, caused by the wicked devices of Haman, Mordecai one day, as usual, came to the gate of the royal palace; at the same time Haman and a host of friends also appeared. They were gleeful and in good spirit, especially when they beheld Mordecai bowed down with grief. Just then the children came from school, and Mordecai ran to meet some of them. Haman, inquisitive why Mordecai ran to these youths, quickly followed behind and overheard the following conversation:

Mordecai: " My son, what was thy lesson to-day?"

First boy: " From Proverbs iii. 25, ' Be not afraid of sudden fear, neither of the desolation of the wicked, when it cometh ; for the Lord shall be thy confidence,'" etc.

Mordecai: " What was thy lesson, my son?"

Second boy: "' Take counsel together and it shall come to naught. Speak ye the word and it shall not stand, for God is with us.'" Isaiah viii. 10.

Mordecai: " And thou, my son, what hast thou learned?"

Third boy: " I have read Isaiah xlvi. 4, 'And

even to your old age I am he; and even to hoary hairs will I carry you: I have made, and I will bear; even I will carry and deliver you.'"

Like a stimulant upon the languid soul acted these words upon the heart of Mordecai. His spirit expanded, and a trembling joy overtook him. He felt like robed in the garment of gladness, with hope of salvation overhanging him. He turned and saw Haman. "Ah!" addressed he him: "hast thou heard these Jewish boys speak of God's word and what they promise? They were inspired with the spirit of God." And Haman was filled with anger and walked off.

—*Esther Midr. Rabbah.*

WHERE GOLD TAKES THE PLACE OF KNOWLEDGE.

The learned and renowned Rabbi Simeon on one occasion visited a wealthy friend in the city of Tyre, and while they were engaged in conversation, the servant entered and asked the host whether he should prepare for dinner from the better or cheaper quality of lentils. " The cheaper quality will do," was the order; and conversation continued. Dinner was announced, and the wealthy host invited the learned guest to the meal; and, as the Rabbi accepted the invitation, the host left him for a moment to give orders to his servants to decorate the dining room pompously. As they entered the appartment, the Rabbi looked with amazement on the glittering metal of gold and silver in such profusion, interspersed with valuable stones; and he addressed himself to his friend, the host, in a jocular manner: " How comes so much splendor of gold, silver and diamonds in the house of one who is so particular in the quality of the lentils he eats? "

" Ah, my friend," responded the host, " ye learned man need no other but your wisdom to make you popular, but we would be unheeded were we not laden with these ornaments which make us conspicuous. Thus we must accumulate them."

—*Midr. Meg. Esther*, 120 *a* and *b*.

OBEDIENCE DUE TO RULERS.

A dispute arose once between the Rabbis Joshua and Gamliel concerning the day of Atonement. Each claimed another day it was to fall on, and one could not convince the other of the certainty of his claim. Rabbi Gamliel, being the Nassi (chief of the rabbis), addressed R. Joshua thus: " I adjure thee, Joshua, to appear before me on the day thou claimest to be the day of atonement with thy staff and thy purse." *

R. Joshua looked despondent and R. Akiba addressed him: " Why is thy countenance so fallen, Joshua? Are not the appointed feasts of God celebrated as annunciated by the Nassi? If then they give correct time or not, and do so advertently or inadvertently, or if they err, it is not our fault."

" Ah, I am consoled, perfectly consoled!" ejaculated Joshua. R. David ben Hirkanos offered another explanation: " From the laws of Moses we infer that we have to abide by the decision of the judge in any age. It says (Deutr. xvii. 9), ' Thou shalt come for adjudication before the judge that will be in *those days.*' Would you perhaps say

---

* Meaning that he should come attired as on ordinary days, as on holidays the Israelites were not allowed to carry with them even a cane, much less the purse which contains the means for traffic, etc.

that *then* the people and times were better? To this Solomon the Wise suggested: ' Say not that the former days were better than these.'" (Eccl. vii. 10.)

On the appointed day R. Joshua announced himself to R. Gamliel: " Behold, I came to thy city, Jabne, with my staff and my purse on the day I claimed as the day of atonement, as thou hast bidden me." R. Gamliel arose from his seat and kissed R. Joshua's forehead, saluting him : " Peace be unto thee, my master and my pupil. My master thou art, for thou hast this time distinctly taught me a noble lesson, and my pupil thou art, for thou hast done as I have bidden thee. Blessed is the generation where the greater men obey the lesser ones if they are the rulers.'

—*Rosh Hashanah,* 25 a.

EVOLUTION OF GOD'S LAW.

A wealthy and learned man had two intimate friends, and as he once departed on a journey, he wished to express his friendship for them, and left to each a measure of corn and a bundle of wool. One of the friends at once proceeded to grind the corn and made dough from the meal, baking it into a palatable bread. The wool he had spun and weaved for a cover on his table.

The other friend preserved the present in the form it was given him.

The learned man on returning home and visiting his friends, the first one invited him to partake of the bread he baked from the corn he received, and showed him the coverlet on his table produced from the wool, and the learned man rejoiced over his energy. The other friend, however; could only show him the corn and the wool as given to him, and the learned man reproved this friend for the lack of energy.

This is the case with the law given on Sinai. We have to prepare it so that it shall become adaptable to the times, to follow it in the original form it has no semblance nor is it palatable.

— *Tana d'be Elia*, 53.

QUALITY BETTER THAN QUANTITY.

Two learned men were occupied in one town as teachers. Both were profound scholars and very wise; one, however, directed more attention to explications of the complicated passages in law and lore, and the other was eloquent in speech; he attracted large audiences with able lectures and splendid discourses. One day, as a multitude was attentively listening to him, he alluded to his contemporary in the following terms: "Do you think that I am more learned than my friend? Let this example tell you:

When you go to a bazaar, you see a dealer in valuable jewels on one side and a dealer in needles on the other, where do you find more people assembled? At the dealer of needles, of course; and why? Because the price of needles is such that everybody can afford to buy them, but not so with the precious jewelry. Thus you will find around the dealer of cheap wares more customers than around the dealer of valuable articles. Therefore, neither makes the multitude a cheap article more precious, nor becomes a rare object depreciated on account of the purchasers being few.

—*Sota*, 40 *a.*

HOSPITALITY.

Raban Gamliel, the great master in Israel, once invited to his house to a festive board some wise rabbins, and as they all were assembled waiting for the festivity to begin, the host arose, signifying his intention to wait on his guests.

The assembled guests emphatically protested against such procedure. The sage, thought they, should not so condescend. He was too high a dignitary, and they begged him to be seated by the table. Rabbi Joshua at last pacified them. He said : "If it is the pleasure of our venerable and revered host to wait on his guests, let him do so. He is surely not greater than was Abraham our progenitor. He, too, attended once to his guests." Inspirited by this explanation, another sage arose, saying : " I know one still greater who waits on his guests' table." " Who, pray, who can be greater than was Abraham ? " inquired several voices. " It is the Holy One, blessed be He," was the reply. " Attends He not to all His creatures? Prepares He not their tables? Let our princely host, therefore, have his pleasure in waiting on his guests."

—Kidushin, 32.

THE DERVISH AND THE INFIDEL.

A man once came to a dervish (a Mohammedan priest) and said: " I wish to lay before you three questions, find me an answer if you can. First, you say that God is everywhere, why can I see him nowhere? Second, you say that the power belongs to God, and all that is done is through Him; how, then, can man be made responsible for his deeds? Third, you say that Satan consists of fire, and that hell is burning fire; as fire cannot harm fire, what punishment is it for Satan to be put into hell?" The dervish unhesitatingly grasped a heavy pitcher and threw it at the questioner's head. The man uttered a lamenting *"yah allah!"* (Lord God) and went before the Kadi (judge) with his bleeding head. The dervish was summoned, and the judge asked him reproachfully whether this was the way a pious man should treat one coming to inquire about religious matters. The dervish replied: " Why, my pitcher was simply the prompt answer to his three questions. He doubted God's existence because he saw Him nowhere, but as soon as he felt the pitcher's weight at his head he shouted *"yah allah!"* which is proof that he found out *Allah's* existence. His second doubt was about man's responsibility for his actions. Now, when my pitcher made his head bleed he did not summon God but me before the Kadi, thus showing his belief conclusively that every man is responsible for his deeds. And I claim to have settled also his third doubt about Satan and hell. My pitcher is clay, and he, as a mortal, is likewise of clay. If then clay can hurt clay, why should not fire be able to hurt fire?" The man forgot his bleeding head on account of the good instruction he had received.

—*Dr. Huebsch's Desc. Orient.*

BE NOT FANATIC.

After Jerusalem was destroyed and the gorgeous temple with it, some superstitious zealots vowed never to taste any more meat and wine. Rabbi Joshua, who then enjoyed a glorious reputation among his brethren, heard of this and sought to convince them of their folly.

"Brethren," said he, "why will you abstain from meat and wine?" "Because, O master," said they, "meat and wine was sacrificed at the altar of God, and how could we now make these our food and drink?'

"Ah," retorted the sage, "ye should then cease to eat bread, for that too was offered in former times."

"Thou, O master, hast spoken right," said the

zealots. " We will likewise abstain from bread, and make fruit our sustenance."

" But from the fruit too the first ripe ones were brought to the altar of God," said Joshua.

" Truly hast thou spoken," said they, " we will only seek such fruit that was not subject to this ordinance."

" But ye must drink neither water, as the ablutions were made with water in the temple in former times," retorted Joshua. The fanatics stood in silence, not knowing what more to say, and the sage continued, " I would not for a moment advise you to forget Jerusalem and cease to mourn for it, but to mourn to excess is unadvisable, and results in no avail."

—*Baba Bathra*, 60 *b*.

THE RIGHTFUL FATHER.

Why doth Israel call God their father.

An orphan girl, forsaken and forlorn, was once rescued from her pitiable condition by a benevolently inclined man, who raised and trained her, as though she were his own child. As she grew older, her foster parent selected her a suitable consort for life, and a notary was summoned to draw up a marriage contract (as was customary among Israelites, and is still so with the orthodox). He asked the damsel her name, which she readily gave; then he asked for her father's name, but she hesitated, gazing sweetly at her benefactor, and the scribe asked why she hesitated? She then sternly replied, in terms that conveyed a deep meaning, "Behold, this noble man is my rightful father!"

In such emphatic terms had Israel declared God as their father after their deliverance from Egypt. "Why," asked God, "have ye forgotten your fathers Abraham, Isaac, and Jacob?" "Nay, we have not," replied Israel, "but we were like orphans, forsaken and forlorn, and Thou hast redeemed us from our pitiable condition and trained us as Thy children, hence we recognize Thee as our rightful father."

—Babboth, 160 *b*.

HOW TO DRINK.

"And Noah began to be a husbandman
and planted a vineyard, and he drank of
the wine and was drunken."—Genesis
ix. 20, 21.

As Noah was planting the vineyard, Satan came
along and inquisitively asked Noah what he was
at, and Noah answered, "I am planting a vineyard." "A vineyard!" asked Satan in astonishment, "what shall a vineyard be good for?" "It
shall bring forth fruit, luscious and sweet, and if
pressed out will produce a refreshing beverage,"
explained Noah. "Ah, indeed!" exclaimed Satan.
"That must be a glorious fruit. Give me a share
in the cultivation, there is plenty of soil;" to which
Noah had no objection, and both were planting
vineyards. Satan devoted a good deal of his time
to this enterprise, and, as he saw one day the little
grapes advancing, he proposed to Noah, "Let us
now consecrate our fruit and all its kindred to the
use of man. Let us endow it with the nature of
mine and your principles." How can that be
done?" asked Noah. "Ah, since thou knowest it
not, I will do the work myself," said Satan and
away he flew. He returned in an instant, grasped
in his left hand an innocent lamb bleating for its
life, and a knife in his outstretched right.

He slaughtered the poor creature and sprinkled its blood over the grapes. This done, he flew away again and returned this time with a roaring lion held by the throat. The terrified Noah witnessed in profound silence this act of consecration, while Satan plunged the knife into the royal beast and sprinkled the flowing blood on the grapes.

"This I have done for your share, addressed he Noah, "and now will come mine; and once more he vanished, returning this time with a frightened ape and a grunting swine. These too he slaughtered and sprinkled their blood on the grapes, and the act of consecration was completed.

Thus it is that the wine and its kindred possess the virtue they primevally received from the hands of Satan. If you drink the first glass you may retain your lamb-like innocence; the second will embolden you like a lion (often to mischievousness); a third glass will make of you a monkey, and a fourth will change you into a swine. Noah not having understood Satan's diabolic consecration, drank more than his own share and became intoxicated.

Moral: Drink, if you drink at all, to imbibe Noah's principles, but leave Satan's alone.

—*Jalkut to Genes.*, 16 a.

THE SWEETEST CONDOLENCE.

Rabbi Jochanan ben Zakai, it is related, lost a hopeful son in prime of life, and his disciples came to offer him condolence, but they found their revered master inconsolable, and the following arguments ensued :

Rabbi Eliezer: " Why, O master, shouldst thou mourn so deeply ? Hath not Adam, the first man, lost his son Abel, one of two in the whole world, and was consoled ; and God blessed him with sons and daughters thereafter ? "

Rabbi Jochanan: " Is not my grief heavy enough ? Why addest thou to it by reminding me of Adam's grief ? "

Rabbi Joshua : " O master, think of Job. He lost all his sons and daughters in one day, and yet his words were, ' God gave and God took, blessed be the name of God.' "

Rabbi Jochanan: " Woe me ! woe me ! Why tellest thou me of Job's bereavement yet ? "

Rabbi Josai : " Did not Aaron lose two sons in one day, dying in the sanctuary, and he kept silence ? "

Rabbi Jochanan : " Woe was unto these righteous men, who could bring me their retribution ! "

Rabbi Simeon : " Did not David lose a beloved

son for whom he mourned bitterly, but was finally consoled?"

Rabbi Jochanan: "Pray cease, for all this cannot console me!" Here Rabbi Eliezer came forward once more, and in his winning way began: "O master, listen to my parable. A monarch once intrusted into the care of one of his subjects a valuable vessel for safe keeping, to be returned when called for. This faithful subject, not knowing when the monarch might reclaim this vessel, yearned and desired to be able to return it in good condition. Thy son, O revered master, like that vessel, full of virtue and piety, was he not entrusted into thy care for safe-keeping by the Monarch of monarchs? And shouldst thou not praise the Lord that thou wert able to return him so pure and so perfect as was thy son? Should this not be your sweetest consolation?" "Ah!" exclaimed Rabbi Jochanan, raising his eyes and hands heavenward, "blessed be thou, Eliezer, from God, thou hast perfectly consoled me!"

—Abdr. Nathan, 14.

ISRAEL'S FAITH IN GOD.

A man once plighted his faith and love to a fair damsel, and they lived together in happiness and contentment. But it so happened that he was called away from her to a long distance, and she was left alone. Long, long, she waited for his return, but he came not. While friends pitied her, her adversaries taunted her with discouraging words: " He will never come back to thee ! " But she would retire into her solitude, and there read and re-read the affectionate letters her spouse wrote to her, in which he vowed and pledged to be faithful and true to her. They comforted and consoled her, and she dried her tears confidently. At last her beloved returned, and he asked her : " Did you ever doubt my faithfulness to thee as others did?" She drew forth the letters he wrote to her, and declared : " How could I have doubted thy faithfulness when I have day by day read thy pledges and vows of everlasting love ? "

This woman is Israel, and the lover is God. She—Israel—was oppressed and derided by nations and people, and mocked in their hope of redemption; but Israel withdrew in retirements of schools and synagogues, where they read and re-read the love letters—Scriptures—God wrote to them, and they believed in the holy and sublime promises they contain ; and in all adverse conditions of life, in their bitterness and in their suffering, they expressed their unshaken faith in God in the words of the Psalmist : " Had not thy law, O God, been my delight, I should have surely perished in mine affliction " (Psalm cxix. 92).

—*Echa Rabba*, 76 a.

THE BENEDICTION.

" Bless me, O master," said Rabbi Nachman to Rabbi Yitzchak, who had enjoyed the hospitality of the former, and was now ready to depart. " Bless me before thou goest."

Rabbi Yitzchak was silent for a moment, then he began : " Listen to me. A man was once travelling in a desert, and as he became weary and tired, he sat down to rest beneath the shadow of a stately tree that bore a luscious fruit, with a brook of crystal-clear water flowing beneath it. Hungry and thirsty, he satiated himself with the fruit, and refreshed his palate with the water. After he rested his weary limbs, and was ready to depart, he began : ' O thou precious tree, wherewith should I bless thee ere I go ? Should I wish that thy fruit shall be prolific and sweet ? Thou art laden with the sweetest fruit. Should I bless thee that thou mayest have abundance of foliage for shade ? Thou hast a beautiful shade. Should

I bless thee that thou shouldst have plenty of water to supply thy root? Behold! there floweth a refreshing stream beneath thee. May it then be acceptable that all the plants coming from thee shall be blessed like thee.' Likewise, my generous host, can I ask, wherewith should I bless thee? That thou shouldst have learning? Thou art a scholar. That thou shouldst be honored and respected? Thou enjoyest the veneration of all that know thee. That thou shouldst become rich? Thou hast all and everything in affluence. That thou shouldst have good children? Thou hast excellent and beautiful children. May it then be acceptable that all thy successors may be like thee, and be blessed like thee."

—Taanith, 5 b.

VANITY.

" A man's pride shall bring him low;
But honor shall uphold the humble in spirit."
—Prov. xxix. 23.

A stag came to a brook to quench his thirst, and beheld in the clearness of the water the reflection of his stature. He was filled with admiration over the beauty of his horns and he rejoiced, feeling very proud; but glancing down at his legs, his countenance fell, and he grieved in his heart over this defect. While he thus stood brooding over this imperfection, he espied some hunters and took to flight.

The legs he felt so bad about, carried him swiftly away, and he would have escaped the hunters, but the horns, in which he so prided himself, caught in some bushes and caused his death. It is the same with man. "His pride shall bring him low, but honor shall uphold the humble in spirit."

—*Oral tradition.*

————

A Canaanite bought a graven image, and put it on the back of his ass to carry it home to his place. On the road all the people that met them bowed down at beholding the image, and the ass thought that these honors were shown to her. This made the animal haughty, and she began to be stubborn, refusing to listen to the master, who took a rod and beat her. So it is with some, who are possessed of riches, on which account they are shown honor; could they but comprehend that the honors shown them are to the wealth they carry they would drop their haughtiness and vain pride; for "a man's pride shall bring him low, but honor shall uphold the humble in spirit."

—*Ibidem.*

POWER OF THE TONGUE.

" Death and life are in the power of the tongue."
                                    --*Prov.* xviii. 21.

Rabbi Simeon had a wise servant, Tobia by
name, who was wont to make the purchases of the
necessaries of the house. The rabbi, to try his
shrewdness one day, told him to bring from market
the best thing he could find, and Tobia brought
home a tongue. The master wondered why his
servant should have selected the tongue as the
best thing. Could he not find many better things?
But before he would put to him these questions,
he decided to send him to market the following
day, with directions to bring the worst thing he
could find; and, lo, the servant again brought a
tongue. "How is this, Tobia?" asked Rabbi
Simeon. "Yesterday I told thee to bring the
best thing thou couldst find in the market,
and thou hast brought home a tongue; to-day I
have told thee to bring the worst, and thou
bringest a tongue again?" "Pardon me, O
rabbi," replied the servant, "is there anything
better than the tongue? And, again, is there anything worse than the tongue? According how
the tongue is employed. Solomon, the king, said
correctly: "Death and Life are in the power of
the tongue'" (Prov. xviii. 21). This convinced the

rabbi of the servant's wisdom, and he promoted
him to a higher servility, viz., the study of law and
lore; and in after years Tobia turned out to be
a great scholar and a shining light.

—*Vajikra Rabba*, 33.

THE POWER OF GOD.

At the time the Jews lived under the Syrian
vassalage, the king one day, after having listened
to the high-priest declaring the power of God,
said: " I honor your God who is so great and
powerful, yet since He permitted me to conquer
you, His people, He, too, must recognize *my*
power and significance. Extend to Him, therefore,
my invitation to a feast I will prepare, and see to
it that He shall attend, or else I will hold you and
your people accountable and make you suffer for
the consequences;" and without giving the high-
priest opportunity to reply the monarch departed.

The day arrived when, in the garden of the
king, situated adjacent to the sea-shore, a great,
an extraordinarily great feast was prepared. The
high-priest was summoned and appeared, but he
assumed a place in a remote corner and engaged
in prayer. The sun shone forth in lustrous brightness, lending grandeur to the occasion, and the
azure sky bore testimony to the sun's illuminative
qualities. The festivity began, and the high-priest

was informed that the king and his court were ready to receive and entertain the God of the Hebrews, but the high-priest, seemingly absorbed in prayer, gave no reply. Again he was reminded of this, but ere he could have answered, were he inclined to, a sudden breeze arose which rapidly grew into a wind; soon it became a hurricane, and finally began to grasp the tent, tables, chairs, and all that was in its way, carrying them into the sea and burying them into its billowy waves. The king became uneasy, and inquired of the high-priest whether he knew the cause of this phenomenon. " My God is approaching," replied he, "and these elements are His servants sent to clear the way before their Almighty Master, as on Mount Horeb in Elijah's time " (see 1 Kings xix. 11, 12). The king trembled, and fearing per-adventure, another gust would come and sweep him along, quickly replied: " Oh, inform your God that He need not come if it is His displea-sure. If He is so powerful I am unworthy of His visit. Ah, if His servants have such might, how great must be the might of the Master!"

Rabboth, 20 *b.*

JUSTICE AND TRUTH.

On that memorable day when the all-wise Ellohim said, "Let us make man in our image," there reigned throughout the celestial domains silence most profound. The angels stood in awe and reverence, attentively listening to the Great Creator, the Holy One, blessed be He!

The angel of truth broke the silence. He stepped to the mercy seat of the Creator, exclaiming: "Create no man, O Most High! It is not hid from Thy omniscient knowledge how false and void of truth the children of man will be."

Thereupon the angel of mercy arose, pleading in accents most touching: "Mercy! have mercy, O Most High! Thou also knowest how kind and charitable the sons of man are destined to be! Create him, therefore, O Lord! create him according to Thy infinite wisdom."

In support of the angel of truth the angel of peace arose, earnestly protesting, "O God, create no man! for strife and discord will hold sway among mankind."

Here the angel of righteousness and justice arose, pleading most suppliantly: " Be righteous and just, O Creator! Cease not to carry out Thy glorious plan and create man.   I will watch over the peace of his children."

The last sound had faded away, and again great silence reigned as before, until the Holy One, blessed be He, created man and gave His dictum.

" Truth shall sprout from the earth, and right-eousness shall look down from heaven !"   Thus it is that truth abides on earth.   Each and every one seeks it, and each and every one finds it in different directions, and what mortal can assert or dispute somebody else's truth justly and right-eously?   That perspicacity abides in heaven.

—*Rabboth*, 8 *a*.

GREATNESS IS NOT IN TUMULT.

A king, once on a tour of inspection through his provinces and domains, was expected to arrive in a certain city, and the streets were thronged with people anxious to see the sovereign.   Rab She-shet, a blind scholarly man, had also turned out among the vast multitude, and that attracted the attention of an individual, who ironically re-marked: " Whole vessels must needs go to the well, but of what necessity will broken ones go ? " Rab Sheshet comprehended that this satire was in-tended for him, and promptly replied : " Wait awhile, friend, and I willconvince thee that I, in my blind state, can see many things better than thou canst with thy eyes open."   Soon a noisy

procession was approaching and the man exclaimed, " The king is coming!"   "Oh, no!" said
the rabbi, " the king is not yet coming.   I will tell
thee when he will come."   Another tumult passed
by, even more noisy than the first, and again the
man called " Here comes the king!"   But the
rabbi again corrected him, " This also is not the
king."   Finally another procession came on, glid-
ing by quietly and in respectful silence.   " Here
comes the king!" exclaimed the blind sage, and it
really was the king, his guard, and his escort.
" How could you tell?" asked the man in astonishment.   " Ah!" responded Rab Sheshet, " great-
ness and excellency appears not with noise and
tumult, but with respect and quietness.   When
God appeared to Elijah on Mount Horeb there
came a storm, but God was not in the storm;
there came fire and earthquake, but God was in
none of these phenomena; but He came in a soft
tender voice, and likewise is it on earth, the greater the man the less his noise."

—*Berachoth*, 58 *a.*

A POINT OF LAW.

A certain wise man from a distant land sent his only son to Jerusalem to study and while there the father took sick, and feeling that his end was approaching, with no other but one of his slaves near him, he willed his entire property to this slave with the proviso that his son should be at liberty to choose one object of inheritance, and the sage expired.

The interment over, the slave hastened to Jerusalem to inform the son of what had transpired, and produced his will, urging the son to make his one choice. The grief to the son was double. He lost an affectionate father and being disinherited. The time allotted for mourning was over and he sought the counsel of his preceptor, complaining bitterly :

" Never have I in the least incurred the displeasure of my father, and, lo, he has disinherited me! One choice he left me and the slave gets all and everything!"

" Not so, my son," retorted the wise teacher. " Cease complaining. Thy father has acted wisely, as is shown by the very will, and mayest thou, his son, be as wise in thy days."

The son could not comprehend wherein lay the wisdom, and the preceptor explained :

" Thy father, no doubt, had none else at his bed-side when he felt the approach of death but this slave. Should he have willed the property to thee the slave might have held thy father's death concealed from thee long enough to plunder all the property, or he might not have informed thee at all. This way the father knew that the slave would think himself master of all, thus he would neither steal from the property nor hesitate to inform thee of thy father's demise, who thinking at the same time that thou wilt know that the property of a slave, like the slave himself, belongs to the master, and thus he left one choice to thee. Choose therefore the slave; and all is thine. But, I see that thou wert too young to compre-hend."

"Ah! I see!" exclaimed the son joyfully. " Yes, I see indeed that wisdom abides with the aged, and understanding in length of days," and acting on the advice of his teacher he became master of his father's estate.

—*Jalkut Kohel.*, 668.

LEARNING BETTER THAN GOLD.

A learned man was a passenger on a vessel where some merchants, carrying rich wares to distant lands, were embarked. They mistook the scholar for a business man, and were endeavoring to find out what merchandise he carried, but as they were unable to do so, they inquired of him personally, and he answered them, "The goods I carry are far more precious and valuable than your goods." The merchants, not understanding his meaning, became ironical, and asked him in satiric manner, "Where are your goods? Do they require no storehouse?" and, searching every nook and apartment of the vessel with no avail, they made the scholar the object of their ridicule. During the voyage the vessel was captured by pirates, who robbed the passengers of all their money and valuables, and ransacked the vessel of all its lading, leaving the merchants destitute and poor. The learned man, as soon as they reached the land, visited the colleges and academies, and his high attainments soon procured him lucrative employment as teacher, and he became renowned and influential, while the merchants had to appeal for aid to charitably inclined people. However pitiable their conditions were, in whatever mournful tale they related their misfortune, they were not believed, and the unfortunate strangers suffered want and privation. They meanwhile, learning of the success of their singular fellow-passenger, condescended to appeal to him for help, as he was acquainted with their misfortune. He, knowing their condition, felt compassion for them, and would by no means have thought to retaliate, but helped them all he could. Yet he could not refrain from teaching them a valuable lesson and he said: " Can ye now see of what my goods consisted? It did not perish like yours. Let this misfortune, therefore, teach you that it is not the quantity but the quality of goods that should be desirable, as you perceive that my goods—my learning—are more valuable than the gold you had."

—Jalkut, 2, 133.

THE PUREST SACRIFICE.

It was customary with Israelites in olden times to bring sacrifice in every event of life. Thus a poor man once, recovering from sickness, sought the temple of God. But he was ashamed to enter as he had no sacrifice with him, and he stood outside listening to the strains of music and the voices of hymnals. He heard the chanting of psalms, and closely listening, he understood the words, " Thou desirest no sacrifice or else I would give it ; thou delightest not in burnt offering.

The sacrifices of God are a broken spirit, and a contrite heart, O God, thou wilt not despise." He thereupon entered among others and prostrated himself before the priest as those did that brought sacrifice. " What wilt thou, my son? " asked him the priest, " hast thou an offering? " " O my father," replied he, " last night a poor widow, mother of children, came to me for help and I gave her the two pigeons which I intended to bring for a sacrifice." " Bring then," said the priest, " an ephah* of fine flour." " Sickness had so impoverished me," pleaded the poor man, " that I have scarcely enough left for my poor hungry children, and I could not even bring this small measure of flour." " Why, then, comest thou hither? " inquired the priest. " Because," said the poor man, " I heard just now sung, ' The sacrifices of God are a broken spirit,' etc. Will God not accept my sacrifice consisting of the prayer, ' O God, be merciful to me, a poor sinner? ' " The priest stretched forth his hands and lifted the poor man from the ground, muttering, " Ay, my son, blessed shalt thou be. Better far than thousands of rivers of oil is thy offering."

— *Tradition.*

---

* A measure of Hebrew origin containing a little more than three pecks.

GAM ZU L'TOBAH.

There lived once a very pious and scholarly man whose name was Nahum the Gam Zu, receiving this surname from his frequent utterance of *gam zu l'tobah* (this is also for the best). Whatever befell him he would utter these words with pious resignation.

In his old age he was disabled and crippled, suffering at times untold agony, and was unable to help himself. One day his disciples visited him, and, seeing his sufferings, asked, "How comes it, O master, that such perfectly righteous man as thou art should be visited so sorely?" "Ah, my sons," said he, woefully, "I fully deserve this, and it is even my own sentence. I was once travelling, and had three asses laden with food, with beverages, and with wearing apparel, when I reached a house. I just wanted to enter, and a poor man cried unto me for help. I heard it and told him to wait till I unloaded my asses. I did go out to him as promised, but it was too late. The poor unfortunate man fell down from sheer exhaustion and expired. I fell on his face and began to pray for mercy and forgiveness, and I have pronounced my sentence, viz.: that the eyes that had no pity should become dim; the hands that extended not the immediate help

should become benumbed; and my feet that hastened not to help should become paralyzed; and
behold, when I was ready to rise, my sentence
took effect, and I had to be carried away. But
gam zu l'tobah—this is also for the best.

—*Taanith*, 21.

THE HEREAFTER.

There lived some time in the thirteenth century
two scholars, both of high culture and unlimited
knowledge; both of profound thought and sound
understanding; and they were greatly attached
to one another, as, from their early youth to
ripe old age, they spent their time together in
the search of knowledge, both religious and profane.

An idea occurred to them to explore all possible
knowledge to find how the body and soul of man
are combined; and, when the body returns to
earth and the soul ascends to Him who hath given
it, how the separation takes place; but all their
efforts and exertions afforded them no satisfac-
tory result, and they concluded to abandon this
fallacious research. They, however, agreed to
enter into a covenant, which they confirmed by
solemn oath, that the one who should die first
should come to his living associate and inform him
of the state in the hereafter. The time came when
one died and was buried by a large concourse of

friends. As they reached the burying ground, the surviving friend requested to halt a while, informing the congregation of the oath that existed between him and the deceased, and the request was granted. The lid was removed from the coffin, but the features of the corpse looked as if he wanted to speak but could not, and the lid was replaced and the body interred.

Time wore on and the surviving friend thought himself entirely forgotten by his demised associate, when one night he appeared to him in a dream begging piteously to be released from his oath, " for," said he, " the great futurity must remain a secret till that *great morning* shall dawn. It is for the welfare of the living not to know the state of the hereafter." He awoke from his dream and released his dead friend from his oath.

—Kav Hajashar, 88.

FILIAL HONOR.

Netina, a heathen living in Ashkalon, had a son named Demah. One day the elders of Israel came to Netina's house to purchase a precious stone he possessed, and which they needed for the ephod of the priest. Its price was a thousand gold shekels. Demah went to his father's chamber to get the stone, but saw him sleeping, his feet resting on the chest the stone was in, and he returned without the jewel rather than to wake his father. The elders departed, thinking meanwhile that he wanted a better price, and soon returned with the resolution to pay ten thousand shekels for it; but Demah declared: "If ye give me this house full of gold and silver I will not wake my father from his sleep." The elders waited a while and Netina awoke. The son then gave them the stone in question. The elders having promised ten thousand shekels, now counted out that amount, but Demah refused to take any more than its former price, saying: "Far be it from me to sell my father's honor."

—*Kidushim*, 31 *a*.

Another remarkably honoring son was Abini. He had five children, but he would not allow them to even open the door for their grandfather when he was present, as he wanted to do him honor himself, and thereby he taught his children filial honor. On one occasion his father wished for a glass of water, and Abini went to get it, meanwhile the father fell asleep, and he stood by his father's side with the glass in his hand until he awoke.

—*Ibid.*

THE COMPUTATION OF LIFE-TIME.

A young man of good qualities and noble propensities departed this life and the following parable was spoken by a sage over his bier: In a gorgeous vineyard many laborers were working, among which was a young man who was conspicuous for his zeal and earnestness in the labor. He worked but a few hours when the master came and took him away to spend the remainder of the day in his own company.

As the laborers came in the evening to receive their wages, the master paid them and the young man alike, at which the laborers were displeased and murmured, "Why should this young man, who worked but a few hours, receive the same wages as we do, who worked all day?" "But this young man," rejoined the master, "has in a few hours done as much as ye have done the whole day." Such is the case with the young man whose premature death we now mourn. He has lived only a few years, but he has in this short time accumulated deserts as many as others have during many years of prolonged life; and now God calls him to himself and will undoubtedly pay him equal reward with those that departed this life in old age.

—*Shir Hashirim Rabba*, 31 *b*.

VERITABLE CHARITY.

Abraham was the most charitable and hospitable man of his age. It is related that he watched for strangers passing by his tent and ran to meet and invite them to partake of his hospitality. For each he had a meal prepared, and when they attemped to thank him for his generosity he would interrupt them, and impress it upon them that it was not he whom they owed thanks, but—"Praise and thank Him," he would say, " who supplies me with a sufficiency that I am enabled to extend to others what I should desire that they would extend to me were I a stranger in their land."

Rabbi Hillel, again, was the most charitable of his age. He was accustomed to send every Friday, and every day preceding a holiday, victuals and money to the poor people in order to enable them to observe the Sabbath and holidays with gladness of heart.

Mar Ukba was another man very charitably inclined. He was once told that a man upon whom he bestowed his charity was an habitual wine drinker (but not a drunkard). " Ah, that I knew not!" said Mar Ukba, and after that he sent him an additional amount to supply him with wine also, as it is written in the holy law (Deut. xv. 8), "Thou shall surely open thine hand wide unto him (speaking of a poor brother), and lend him *sufficient* to appease his want.

—*Kethuboth,* 67 *b.*

WHY GOD DESTROYS NO IDOLS.

Some philosopher asked Raban Gamaliel, " why does your God not destroy the idols, if he forbids idolatry?" The sage replied in a parable: "A monarch had once a wayward son, who in his mischievousness had the audacity to name his dog after his father. Whom should the father have punished, the dog or the son?" "But," asserted the philosopher, "if the idols were destroyed, idolatry would not exist." "Yes," replied the sage, "if the objects of worship were only such that are otherwise useless to the world ; but some of these objects are of the most vital importance to the entire human family." "But," continued the philosopher, "why not destroy those objects which are useless and are still objects of idolatry?" "Because," explained Gamaliel, "if the useless objects, sun, moon, stars, etc., were destroyed, the worshippers of the spared idols would then for certainty accept that their gods are the true ones. It is therefore the will of God to let them all exist. Listen to this parable: A man once stole some wheat and sowed it into his field; should the wheat, because it was stolen, not have grown? Nay, the wheat must vegetate, the earth perform its natural functions, but the thief who stole the wheat deserves punishment."

—Aboda Zara, 54 and 55.

METHOD OF TEACHING.

Rabbi Akiba said: A man is in duty bound to instruct his pupil until the latter becomes thoroughly acquainted with the subject of instruction, and this we infer from the ways of Moses. He instructed first Aaron the command he received from the Lord, then came the sons of Aaron and he instructed them in the hearing of their father. Then came the elders and he instructed them in the presence of the priests; then came the whole congregation and he instructed them in the presence of the priests and elders. By this method Aaron heard the lessons four times, his sons three times, the elders twice, and the whole congregation once. Hereupon Moses left and Aaron repeated the lesson before the whole assembly. Then Aaron left and the sons repeated the lesson, and now Aaron's sons left and the elders rehearsed the lesson. In this wise every one received the same instruction four times over. From this Rabbi Eleazar ben Azariah infers that a teacher must repeat a lesson with his pupil at least four times.

—*Erubim*, 54 *b.*

RESPECT THE CUSTOM.

Ever govern yourself according to prevalent custom. This we learn greatly from Moses who when in heaven abstained from food and drink, because such is the custom in celestial domains; while the angels when visiting Abraham regarded the custom of man, and they ate and drank.—Bab. Mez., 110 *b*.

In Maase d'rab Eliezer it is expressed somewhat like this:

Where others weep beware of merry-making,
  Nor shalt thou, when all are gleeful, weep;
And why shouldst thou when others sleep be waking,
  Or be waking when all others sleep?
Be not thou seated when others have to stand;
  Nor stand thou alone when others sit—
Be ever guarded, at whate'er place or land,
  Not to do what custom won't permit,
Only swerve from this if must be;
But be sure you're acting justly.

CONVERT YOUR OWN BEFORE YOU CONVERT OTHERS.

The following dialogue took once place between an idolater and Rabbi Joshuah ben Karchah:

Idolater: "Is it not written in thy book of laws 'follow the majorities,' and why do ye not follow us, are we not far in the majority?"

Rabbi: "Have you any children?"

Id.: Oh, me! that thou remindest me of my trouble!"

Rabbi: "Why, hast thou no children?"

Id.: "Aye, I have children, but day by day there is quarrel amongst them on account of their belief. Each believes differently."

Rabbi: "And why makest thou no peace amongst them?"

Id.: "Would I could, but they listen not to me."

Rabbi: "If then thou art unable to pacify thy own children, why direct thy efforts towards us?" The rabbi's disciples listening to this now spoke:

Disciples: "Thou hast, O master, defeated him with a straw and a mere broken reed."

Rabbi: "Not so, my sons. Is not God with all people and nations, and are they not in the great majority? But Israel is a singular people. They say and believe 'The Lord is our God, the Lord is One!'"

—*Rabboth,* 169 *b.*

SPIRIT OF ADVANCEMENT.

Rabbi Judah Hanassi, the editor of the Mishna, had on one occasion given privilege to do a certain thing which theretofore was considered religiously forbidden. His friends and relatives consequently assembled and reproached him severely. "Why," said they in alarm, "what thy forefathers and ancestors have declared forbidden venturest thou to make permissible?" But he palliated them, bringing inferences from holy writ. "For instance," declared he, "Hezekiah destroyed the serpent of copper which Moses had made in the wilderness because Israel had idolized it. How could he destroy what Moses made and what his ancestors left unabolished? Have not

Assa and Jehoshaphat destroyed all idols, and yet thought not of the serpent which Israel now had worshipped? They have overlooked it and Hezekiah deemed it proper to remedy an old error. Likewise can we infer that, if anything becomes idolatrous or absurd, notwithstanding our ancestors have hallowed it, we shall discard it and accept amendments made by learned men who understand to correct old errors."

—*Chulin*, 6.

HUMANE LAW.

Rabba bar bar Channah once hired two laborers to haul him home some wine, and as accident had it, one of the vessels got broke and the contents spilled. Rabba demanded indemnity for his loss and took the robes of the laborers as security. The unfortunate hirelings went to Rav (or Rabbi Aba in full) and laid their grievance before him. The kind rabbi summoned the employer of these men and urged him to return their garments.

" By what law canst thou judge thus?" asked Bar bar Chanah. " By the sacred dictum in Prov. ii. 20, ' That thou mayest walk in the way of good men ; ' " and the garments were restored unto their owners. But the plaintiffs, pressed by poverty, pleaded further: "O Rabbi, we are poor, and if we should receive no wages to-day our wives and children will suffer for bread." The rabbi in soft tones addressed Bar bar Chanah: " O give them their wages." " What!" retorted the owner of the wine, "they have incurred a loss on me and I shall yet pay them wages? What law is that?" "The same just and humane law as the former. It is written (ibid.): 'And keep the paths of the righteous.'"

—*Baba Mezia,* 83 *a.*

LET HARD WORK NOT SCARE YOU.

A certain king had in his garden a very deep cavity penetreating into the ground so deep that the bottom was scarcely visible. One day he desired that cavity filled up and hired some laborers who were to collect earth and other loose material sufficient for the work ; but some at seeing the deep cavity were scared and asked, " How is it possible to fill that immense depth up?" But others more considerate calmed them by saying: " What does it matter if the cavity is ever so deep? we are paid by the day and we ought to be glad that we found employment. Let us do our duty and that is all there is expected of us."

Likewise do some men say, " Oh, how vast is God's law! It is deeper than the sea and higher than the sky. How many precepts and how many doctrines! How can we comply with them all? But the Holy One, blessed be He, demands of us no impossibilities. Let us do our duty and comply with what we can, and it will be acceptable in the eyes of God.

—*Jalkut,* 271 *b.*

A TIME TO HONOR MAN.

A pious man was once travelling and as the tim, arrived for prayer he halted and performed his devotion. Just then a magnate came along and saluted him, but the praying traveller did not return the salutation until he finished his prayer. The magnate waited patiently and asked him then : " Is it not written in thy scriptures, 'keep thy soul very carefully?' Suppose when I saluted thee and thou didst not respond, I would have cut off thy head, whose fault would it have been?" "My lord," replied the pious Jew, "suppose thou wouldst stand in conversation with a king or sovereign and some one would pass by and salute thee, wouldst thou turn from the king and return the salute?" "Ah, that I could not," said the magnate, "because woe would be unto me to slight the king in such manner." "If then a king, who is mortal like we are," explained the traveller, "would punish thee for feeling himself slighted, how much more careful should we be in reverence of a king who is the king of all the kings, before whom I stood when thou hast approached me?" The magnate was satisfied with the explanation and allowed the traveller to pursue his journey unmolested.

—*Berachoth*, 32 *b*.

ENVY IS NOT PROFITABLE.

"And God made two great luminaries; the greater luminary to rule by day, and the smaller luminary to rule by night."
—Gen. i. 16.

Why is it first stated two great luminaries, and then one greater and one smaller? When God created the sun and the moon they were equal in brightness, but the moon, being envious that her sister's brilliancy should equal hers, asked in accents of jealousy: "What is it necessary for that two kings should wear the same crowns?" No sooner had she expressed this than she became pale and dark with not even as much brightness as a star possesses. She at once repented and began to pray for tender mercies. Her prayer was responded to by an angel of God: "Because thou wert envious of thy sister's equal glory with thine, thou wert entirely deprived of lustre; but thy prayer was heard and, therefore, thou shalt still shine, but only at night and through the light borrowed from the sun, and that according to how she shall pass thee."

—*Rabb.*, 8 *a.*

INDISCREET HELP.

A Babylonian, once travelling, seated himself on the wayside to rest and saw two birds fighting with one another, and one grasped the other and killed it. The same moment the living bird de-

scended, picked a certain grass, and touched with
it the face of the dead bird, and it came to life
again.   The traveller seeing this, took with him
from the same grass, thinking to raise all the dead
buried in the land of Israel.   Thus he resumed
his journey.   On the road he found a dead fox, he
touched the lifeless animal with this grass and,
behold, it came to life, arose, and leaped away.
He travelled further and he came to a high rock,
there he saw a dead lion.   He applied to him also
this grass, and the lion too arose, and lived, but at
the same time grabbed his resuscitator and tore
him to pieces.   This is as Solomon has it: " As
to bind a precious stone in a sling " (Prov. xxvi. 8).

—*Vayikra Rabba*, **22**.

POWER OF SPEECH.

Two able logicians were once displaying their
talent before Emperor Hadrian, one endeavoring
to excel the other.   The first in forcible terms il-
lustrated the power of speech, what it can effect
socially, intellectually, commercially, and in every
branch of life ; while the other took his position in
favor of silence.

He began to illustrate the advantages of silence,
when the first stepped forward and slapped him in
the mouth, stopping him from proceeding with his
argument.

The emperor, somewhat displeased, addressed
the first : " What argument do you call that, pre-

venting your opponent from speaking, in such a manner?" "Sire," retorted he, "have I not argued the advantages of speech? And now comes my antagonist desiring to substantiate his argument, which is on silence, with speech, thus using my own weapon to fight me." He was the victor.

—Jalkut, 212 *b.*

SINGULAR UPRIGHTNESS.

Rab. Safra had a valuable jewel for sale, for which some merchants offered him five gold pieces, but he had asked for it ten, which the merchants were unwilling to give, and they departed. After mature consideration, Rab Safra came to the conclusion that the stone was not worth more than five gold pieces, and decided to sell it for that. In the mean time, the merchants needing the stone concluded to pay the price asked for it, and returned next day to R. Safra's house. "We came," said they, "to offer you two more pieces for the jewel than we offered yesterday, will you let us have it?" R. Safra at this time stood in prayer and would not answer. The merchants mistook this silence for his refusal of the offer and expressed their willingness to give him ten pieces, as he asked yesterday. As R. Safra concluded his prayers he told the merchants that he decided to sell it for five pieces and that he would take no more under any circumstances.

—Baba bathra, 88 *a.*

LIE AND VICE.

When Noah had finished the ark and was admitting into it all and everything as commanded by God, Lie also came and asked for admittance; but Noah refused her admittance on the ground that he must admit a pair of every living thing. Lie, thus turned away from the ark, went in search after a mate and, after considerable pursuit, found Vice. She tried to induce him to go with her, but he would not associate with Lie. They finally came to the agreement that Lie would give all her profits she will ever make to Vice, and with these conditions they presented themselves before the ark as a pair and were admitted. After the deluge was over and they left the ark, Lie repented of her agreement, but she could impossibly alter it; and so it remained forever. The psalmist has it in these terms: "Behold, he travaileth with iniquity and has conceived mischief, and brought forth falsehood." (Pslm. vii. 14.)

—*Jalkut Gen.*, 14 *a.*

WHY ISRAEL WAS CHOSEN BY GOD.

A certain king had among others a purple robe of which he constantly reminded his servant to take special care. This reminder came so often and so repeatedly that the servant's curiosity was aroused, and he ventured to ask: "Why, O king, should this robe be taken more care of than the hundreds of other robes?" "Because," said the king, "this robe is the dearest to me, for I wore it on that day I was placed on my throne."

Likewise said Moses to the Holy One, blessed be He, "Why, O God, speakest thou to me of Israel so repeatedly and continually? Are not all nations thy children?"

"They are," said the Lord, "and I love all, which is manifest from the grace and mercy I extend to all, but I have chosen Israel to be my *first-born son* (see Exodus iv. 22) because they were the first who recognized me and proclaimed my kingdom and existence upon earth."

—Jalkut, 102 *b*.

ISRAEL'S SACRIFICE.

Why did God prescribe Israel to offer sacrifices? Not perhaps that He feeds on or enjoys sacrifice. Nay, God says to Israel, believe ye not that sacrifices shall have the power to appease my wrath or bend my will, or that ye do me a favor; for not according to my will are your sacrifices, but according to your desires. This parable will explain: The son of a king habituated himself to eat and drink outside of his father's house, associating with undignified companions and learned ill manners. The king then said, my son, thou canst eat and drink all thou desirest, but eat and drink at my house. Thus it is with Israel: they were accustomed in Egypt to offer sacrifice, as did the Egyptians to their idols, and the Lord said, let them have their pleasure in sacrificing, but let it be to me, to the true God.

—*Menachot*, 110; *Jalkut*, 176 *b*.

THE SYNAGOGUE GOD'S ABODE.

According to rabbinic literature, the divine law is God's daughter, hence:

A monarch having had only one daughter gave her as a wife to a good man. As the wedding, and the feast connected with it, was over, the husband desired to leave and take his wife with him. The monarch addressed him thus: " My daughter I cannot withold from thee, and it is hard for me to part from her; yet go in peace, but wheresoever ye shall dwell have a little appartment set aside for me, where I can dwell with you from time to time." Thus gave God His beloved daughter— the divine law—to Israel and said: " I cannot withhold her from you, and it is hard for me to part with her; take her then, but consecrate a little place for me, wherever ye shall dwell, and I will from time to time come and dwell there with you."

—*Rabb.*, 151 *a*.

THE SABBATHIC ANGELS.

Rabbi Josai ben Jehudah taught:

When on Sabbath eve (Friday after sundown) the pious worshipper leaves the synagogue, two angels, one good and one evil, join and accompany him home. Arrived at the house, it depends upon the arrangement of the house as to which angel shall bless him. If the house has a truly sabbathic appearance, *i. e.*, illuminated for the occasion and edibles prepared accordingly, the angel of good joyfully exclaims: May thy house enjoy many such Sabbaths, to which the angel of evil, though reluctantly, has to respond amen. But when the house is neglected and indifferently arranged as to sabbathic appearance, the angel of evil joyously calls out: May thy Sabbaths ever thus appear, and the angel of good amidst sighs and tears has to respond amen.

—Sab., page 119 *b*.

THE SURETIES OF GOD'S LAW.

As Israel was ready and willing to accept the law from Sinai, the Lord asked for surety that they would keep and respect it, and they offered their ancestors as surety ; but the Lord said they are insufficient, inasmuch as they themselves were defective. " Abraham, when I have promised him Canaan for inheritance, he asked, whereby shall I know it? (Gen. xv. 8) as expressing doubt. Isaac loved Esau who was antagonistic to my existence. Jacob deceived his father."

" May then," said Israel, " our future prophets become sureties for us." " Neither can I accept your prophets," said the Lord. " They, too, will have often disobeyed my words."

" Let then our children become sureties," said
Israel. " Ah! them I accept with delight," said
the Lord. " They shall safely keep my ever existing law."

TOLERANCE.

The wise men of Jabne (a name Jerusalem was
often called by Talmudic writers) often made
declarations teaching the people the noble trait of
tolerance, and here is one specimen that came
from and was indorsed by all, though spoken
as by one man :

" I am, like my neighbor, God's creature, but
he chooses to live and work in the country while
I prefer the city. I rise a little later to seek my
welfare and gain, and he rises earlier   toattend to
his interest ; but as he seeks not my disadvantage
so must I not seek to injure his interest or standing. And should I imagine myself nearer to God
because, perchance, my occupation is to promote
knowledge and his is not ? Oh, no ! God esteems
and rewards all, who do little or do much, according to their desert, and according to their
intentions."

—Berachoth, 17 *a.*

WHY WOMAN WAS MADE FROM A RIB.

God hath not made Eve of the head part of
Adam that she shall not be headstrong; nor of the
eyes that she shall not see everything and become

vain ; nor of the ear that she shall not listen to everything and become an eavesdropper ; nor of the mouth that she shall not speak too much and become a tale-bearer ; nor of the heart that she shall not be envious ; nor of the hand that she shall not reach for everything and become extravagant ; nor of the foot that she shall not be addicted to running around and entice others or be enticed to temptation and lust, but from the rib was she made, a part of the body which is ever hid from sight, so that she too shall not be exposed to excess but remain in respectable attitude to the public.

— *Rabboth*, 20 *b.*

OF ALL, GOD IS MOST MERCIFUL.

Ask wisdom what punishment shall be imposed on a sinner, and she answers: " Evil pursue the sinners " (Prov. xiii. 21).

Ask prophecy what punishment shall be imposed on the sinner, and she answers : The soul that sinneth shall die " (Ezekiel xvii. 20).

Ask the law (a name the Pentateuch is known by, viz., Torah) what punishment shall be imposed on a sinner, and she answers: " Let him bring a trespass offering and it shall atone for him " (Lev. v. 7).

Ask God what shall befall the sinner, and He, in simple and merciful expression, says: " Repent and live " (Ezekiel xviii. 32).

—*Jalkut*, 71 *a.*

GOLDEN ADVICE.

The disciples of Rabbi Eliezer visited him when he was sick, and they begged him to teach them the path of life. The sage told them but a few words, viz., " Guard the honor of your associates, and when ye pray be mindful before whom ye pray."

Rabbi Jochanan ben Zakai when he lay sick and was expected to die, his disciples paid him a last visit, and they begged that he would bless them. The dying master in feeble voice said: "Oh, may it be acceptable that your fear of God may be as the fear of man." " Should we not fear God more than man?" asked his disciples with astonishment. " Ah!" said Rabbi Jochanan, " I were satisfied if you would take such care not to sin against God as you take care not to offend man."

— Berachoth, 28.

A BENEVOLENT THIEF.

A hypercritic once expressed to Rabban Gamaliel that God was a thief because he stole a rib from Adam while he was asleep. The daughter of the rabbi begged permission to answer, and she said: "A thief came into my apartment and stole silver cups, replacing them, however, by golden ones. What would you do in the case?

" What would I do?" asked the critic, " why, I would be perfectly satisfied." " Well, then," responded the damsel, "did not God do likewise? He took from Adam a mere rib and left him for it a wife."

—*Sanhedrim*, 39 *a*.

SPAN OF LIFE.

Man is like that vegetation which sprouts from the ground as a tender plant, and gradually grows until at last it withers away and perisheth. This, O man, should teach thee to live pleasurably, enjoying the wealth that is at thy command while thou livest; for, consider, how long may that be? Life may become extinct much sooner than expected, and death is sure to come. What matters it then if the heirs will inherit a little more or a little less? Thou, O man, knowest not even how they will prize it, whether they will make good use of it or squander it.

—*Erubim*, 54 *a*.

THE BALM OF LIFE.

A merchant selling spices, and travelling around visiting cities, passed once a certain street calling aloud, "Who wants to buy balm of life? Who wants to buy balm of life?" Rabbi Janai hearing this ran out and addressed him, "Pray, show me that balm of life you offer for sale, for I desire to live." And the merchant replied: "Nay, my master! not for thy sake have I uttered those words." But Rabbi Janai insisted for the precious balm, and the man drew forth a book of Psalms showing him the words: "Who is he that desireth life? Let him keep his tongue from evil, and his lips from slander. Depart from evil and do good" (Psalm xxxiv. 12).

—*Rabboth*, 182 *b*.

FIRE OF RELIGION.

Why, asks a *medrash* (commentary), has the Lord proclaimed His law on Sinai amidst fire? The answer is: because fire was the allegorical portraiture of its attributes.

Those that stay far from it are in darkness and cold; those that approach it too closely become dazzled and overheated, but those that keep at proper distance from it derive the benefit. So it is with religion. Keep aloof from it and your heart will freeze from inhumanity, and your morals will be in the dark. Have too much religion, you will become overheated with fanaticism. The proper religion is that which will mark you a man, a benefit to others as to yourself.

—*Chulin*, 6.

INJUDICIOUS PRAYER.

" Thou shalt not covet."—10th. Com.

King Midas, of Phrygia, it is related, was very avaricious, and at one time he prayed to his god to grant him that everything he would touch should turn into gold, and his prayer was granted. Every thing he touched became instantly gold, and Midas thought himself the happiest mortal on earth. But, oh, how soon he saw how fallacious his prayer was. Amidst plenty of gold starvation stared him in the face, as even the food he was to eat changed to gold by his touch. He then humbly implored: "O my God, deliver me from the curse of gold, that I may again enjoy my daily food."

—*Kidushim*, 36 *a*.

WHY THE DECALOGUE WAS GIVEN IN THE WILDERNESS.

If the Lord had revealed His law unto Israel in a certain country, that country would have raised itself proudly above the others, thinking itself more distinguished than all lands in the universe; therefore the Lord chose a wilderness for His divine revelation. He furthermore revealed His law in the wilderness to indicate that as the inhabitants of a wilderness are free (not governed by despots or monarchs), so shall those observing the law be free. The most obvious reason, however, is, that as the law was given in the wilderness, it was adapted to no certain country and. people; but every people and every country should become possessors of God's law.

—*Jalkut*, 240 *b*.

RELIGIOUS LOVE.

" And thou shalt love the Lord thy God," indicates that we must endeavor to make ourselves beloved by all the creatures of God whom we love; to keep far from sin and deceit. Not only as much as concerns the Jews, but also Gentiles and everybody. He who will steal from an idolater will steal from a godly man also; he who will swear falsely against one will do it against the other; who will deceive one will deceive the other; who would murder a Gentile would not hesitate to murder a Jew neither. The law on Sinai was given not to profane, but to sanctify God's name.

—Jalkut, 267 *a.*

A FAITHFUL SHEPHERD.

As Moses was keeping the sheep of his father-in-law in the wilderness, one day a lamb ran away from the flock, and Moses went in search of it. He found it beneath a shady foliage at a brook quenching its thirst, and Moses gently lifted the little creature into his arms, speaking to it tenderly: " O poor little lamb ! is it thirst that drove thee hither?" and carried it back to the flock. God then said: " Such faithful shepherd art thou ; then be thou the shepherd of my flock Israel. I know that thou wilt feed them with love and mercy; " and Moses became the shepherd of Israel.

— Shemoth Rabba, 120 *a.*

CONSTANCY.

Akabya ben Mahlalel often expressed his opinion in opposition to the rabbins. They endeavored to induce him to recall his doctrines, but he remained immovable. On one occasion they offered him the dignified office of chief of the academy if he would but withdraw his opinion, but he firmly declined the offer saying: " Rather would I he called all days of my life ignorant than appear a sinner before God for one hour. Would not the people say that I have resigned my conviction for the sake of honor?"

—Edioth, 5.

SABBATH VS. WEEK DAYS.

Rabbi Akiba was once asked by Gov. Turnusrupis, " Why are your Sabbath days considered more holy than ordinary days?" " Why art thou considered more eminent than the other people?" asked him Rabbi Akiba in return. " Because," replied the governor, "I am appointed by the king to be governor over them." " So has the Lord our God, who is greater than all kings, appointed the Sabbath day to be sanctified more than the rest of days of the week," concluded Rabbi Akiba.

— Tanchuma, 33.

KEEP ALOOF FROM THE TEMPTER

"An Amonite and Moabite shall not enter the congregation of God."—*Deut.* xxiii. 4.

Although the Egyptians and the Edomites inflicted upon Israel heavy wounds with weapon and oppression, yet Moses bids not to hate them, because we were strangers with the Egyptians in their land, and Edom is from the same descent as we are, but the Amonites and Moabites have tempted and seduced Israel to sinfulness; therefore it is commanded not to admit them in the congregation of God.

— *Jalkut*, 245 *b*.

THE MAGNITUDE OF REPENTANCE.

"And the Lord set a mark upon Cain," etc.
— *Gen.* iv. 15.

After Cain slew his brother Abel and the Lord took him to task, he repented, on which account the Lord set a mark on him—a mark of security. As Adam saw him, he was astonished and asked, "How could you appease the wrath of the Lord and obtain His gracious protection?" "I have sincerely repented, and the Lord in His infinite goodness showed me mercy." "Repented! woe unto me!" moaned Adam, "why knew I not how precious in the sight of God repentance is? I also might have turned away His wrath."

— *Jalkut*, 11 *a*.

GOD IS EVERYWHERE.

An idolater in conversation with Rabbi Josai said to him : " My gods are mightier than thy God, and I prove it to you by the very fact that Moses, when his God appeared to him in the thorn bush, hid his face, but when he saw the serpent, which is one of my gods, he fled from it." "Ah!" answered the Hebrew sage, "from our God we cannot flee as from yours, for he is on heaven and on earth, on sea and on dry land; but from thy god we can flee and be delivered."

— *Rabboth*, 121 *b.*

A GENEROUS REVENGE.

Rabbi Meier at one time dwelt at quarters surrounded by such disagreeable neighbors that at one occasion he felt so annoyed that in his forgetfulness he exclaimed: "I wish God would take them!" Beruriah, his pious wife, promptly admonished him thus: "Why should God take the sinner? Why not rather the sin? Were it not wiser to say: would that God would inspire the hearts of these wicked neighbors that they might become better?"

—*Berachoth*, 10 *a.*

WHO ARE THE CHILDREN OF GOD?

A certain king had a son who was exceedingly desirous of being recognized as the king's son whithersoever he went, and the father told him: "If you so desire to be known as my son, attire yourself in my purple robe, put my crown on your head, and all will at once recognize thee."

Thus said the Lord to Israel: "Accept ye my law and observe it faithfully, and all will recognize you as my children."

—*Rabb.*, 298 *b*.

THE ALTAR A PROMOTER OF LIFE.

As holy writ informs us (Exod. xx. 25), the altar was to be built without iron instruments. Why? Because iron furnishes material to shorten man's life, while the altar was to be the means of reconciling man with God and promoting life. The material, therefore, that furnished instruments of murder should not touch God's altar which was to lengthen life.

—*Midoth*, 34.

A VIRTUOUS WOMAN.

—*Prov.* xxxi. 10-31.

A virtuous woman, oh, who can find?
Far above rubies is precious her kind.
The heart of her husband in her confides;
Thus spoil of riches with them e'er abides.
Goodness untainted by evil, this wife
Acquires for her husband throughout her life.
For wool and for flax she seeketh so fain,
With two willing hands to work them to gain.
Food she procureth from laudable source,

Like merchandise vessels from distant shores.
Early she riseth—the night's not yet o'er,
To see to her house, her maids to care for.
With provident care she purchaseth lands,
Planting a vineyard with toil of her hands.
Her loins girt with strength, her arms firmness bear;
She buyeth her goods inspected with care.
From burning her light all night doth not cease—
Handling the distaff and spindle with ease,
The wants of the poor her hands do appease.
Of snow for her household she's not afraid;
For they are in robes of scarlet array'd.
Tapestried covers herself she prepares;
Dresses of silk and scarlet she wears.
Her husband is well known within the gates,
Where with the wise of the land he debates.
He selleth the linen which she has made,
And girths she prepares supplieth the trade.
Her days end in joy—her lips wisdom say;
Precepts of kinds her tongue doth display—
Even her garments do firmness betray.
She keeps of her household due oversight;
Of idleness void she eateth her diet.
Her children, duly to praise her, arise;
With commendation her husband replies.
Many a daughter has virtuously done,
Yet thou excellest them all—ev'ry one!
Grace is deceitful and beauty is vain;
The God-fearing woman's praise will remain.
Oh, give her the honor she reaps by her hands!
Her acts be her praise in the gates of all lands!

SOLOMON AND ASHMEDAI.

The gorgeous temple of Solomon, Scripture tells (1 Kings vi. 7) us, was built without hammer or any instrument of iron, which gave the wise king no little anxiety ; and it was no common undertaking to accomplish, what no human being had accomplished before him. Consequently, he one day assembled his counsellors to devise ways and means as to how the house of God should be built. He addressed them thus :

"Ye know that the Lord commanded through Moses that His altars should be built from stone without iron tools (Deut. xxvii. 5) and I am about to erect a house to the sanctity of the One God, can you advise me how stones could be cut without iron?" "We can only inform thee, O King," replied the counsellors, "that there exists a small insect called *Shamir** which Moses already employed in making the Ephod. Its sharpness no stone, however hard, can withstand." "Where," asked Solomon, "can this creature be found?" "That," said they, "we cannot tell thee. But

---

* Tradition relates that this minute insect was created with other things (ten in number) at twilight on the sixth day of creation ; and derived its name, no doubt, from the nature of its office, as Shamir in Hebrew is a sharp point.

thou, O King, hast power even over spirits,* command, therefore, that a demon pair be brought before thee, and torture them, if necessary, until they disclose its whereabouts." Forthwith two demons were conjured, and Solomon demanded that they disclose the abode of the Shamir, but they declared, " We know not where the Shamir abides, but Ashmedai, our king, may perchance know all about it." " Where can your king be found?" was the inquiry. " He resorts to a remote mountain," was the reply. " There he dug a deep cavity which he occasionally fills with clear water wherewith to quench his thirst daily. This cavity is covered with a stone and sealed with his signet, so that nobody should open it in his absence without his detection. Daily he visits the heavens and makes a circuit of the earth to espy everything, and at dusk he returns to his mountain to refresh himself with the pure water. He then reseals the cavity carefully and flies away again to ramble in the darkness of the night;" and they described the whereabouts of the mountain.

Benajah, the son of Jehojada, was now called and entrusted with the mission of capturing the demon king. For this purpose Solomon supplied him with his own signet ring and a chain both

---

* This idea is an erroneous inference from the passage in Eccl. ii. 8, where Solomon says, " I had *shedo* and *shedoth*," man singers and women singers, but somehow or other these words were confounded with the Talmudic *shedah* and *shedin*—he and she demons —which caused the misapplication of acceding to Solomon the power over the demons.

bearing the engraving of the ineffable name of the Most High, so peculiarly executed that it possessed the power of enchantment; several casks of wine were also provided and bundles of wool, then the instruction; and Benajah departed to seek the demon chief. After considerable travel and search, he found the spot exactly as described, and he immediately went to work according to instructions by Solomon which were these: He undermined the cavity, thus drawing off the water, then fastened the hole with the wool and covered it to an unrecognizable extent. Then he dug a hole above this and emptied the wine into the cavity, thus replacing the water. This hole he also closed like the lower one and withdrew to a neighboring tree which he climbed, thence to watch and await the arrival of Ashmedai. At his usual hour he arrived and inspected the mountain all around carefully, then looked at the seal which he found intact, and he broke it. He rolled away the stone and was about to sip the fluid when he sprang to his feet, exclaiming "Wine! how came it hither? Nay, 1 will not drink it, for 'wine is a mocker' (Proverbs xx. 1), and I shall not become a derision!" This, however, was only said, for his burning thirst bid him otherwise. Instead of leaving in quest of pure water he lingered there, smelling again and again the fragrant odor issuing from that glorious wine until temptation* overtook him;

---

* This is intended for a lesson that we shall not, like the demon, despise a thing and then still linger around it until temptation shall overtake us, and we become a prey to misery. Especially with the

and he quenched his thirst with the intoxicating beverage. His thirst demanded more and more until he lay prostrated on the ground intoxicated and unconscious. Silently Benajah descended from the tree, approached the drunken chief and laid the enchanting chain on his neck. How raged Ashmedai when he awoke and found himself in chains, but Benajah called out, " Waste not thy anger and thy strength, for, behold, thou art fettered by a holy name!" Ashmedai glanced at the chain, and, recognizing the fact that he was in the power of Benajah, he became calm and resistless, and permitted himself to be led away. Inwardly, however, his rage was burning, and on the way he played sad havoc with anything and everything that chanced to be in his way. Trees, fences, houses and everything he touched fell to the ground.

He was about to approach a poor widow's hut, when she came out begging him piteously to spare her humble abode, to which he yielded, and stepped aside, at the same time he hurt his arm, and he scornfully cried, " I ought to have known that ' a soft tongue breaketh the bone'" (Prov. xx. 16).

Farther on a blind man was straying from his path and would have become entangled in a thorny bush, when Ashmedai, unsolicited, sprang to his rescue and led him into the right way. This astonished Benajah and he asked, " How is it that

---

cup ; hover not around it, if you know that it is not compatible with your constitution or habit.

erst you were sorry that you spared the poor widow's house, while here you were so willing to assist?"

"Ah," replied Ashmedai, "not for his sake, but for my own benefit have I helped him. I have heard it announced in heaven that he is a good and pious man, and any one that will bestow on him a favor will reap great reward; hence I have served him, to share myself the benefit of reward."

Further on they met a drunkard who in his drunkenness was off the road, and another step would have thrown him into a deep pit and probably cost him his life. Ashmedai leaped to his assistance and put him on the straight road.

"Why hast thou shown this favor to this man?" asked Benajah. "This man," replied Satan, "I have helped to his own disadvantage. He is a corrupt man, and whatever little reward he deserves, I wanted him to obtain in this world."*

On their journey they arrived at a place where a wedding was consummated and Ashmedai began to weep aloud. "Why weepest thou when all others are rejoicing?" asked him Benajah. "I weep, because I cannot rejoice when others are jubilant,† but in thirty days the twain will be parted by death, then will I rejoice."

---

* Tradition has it that many reap their reward here, and will have so much less in the future world, and *vice versa*, according to their deserts.

† A demon is always contrary, of course; and this allegory is to illustrate the absurdity of such trait, and teaches us to train our manners differently. Endeavor to harmonize with your fellow-men,

Onward they travelled, and on the road they overheard one wishing he could get a pair of sandals to last him seven years, and Ashmedai laughed aloud. " Why laughest thou ?" inquired Benajah. " Shouldn't I laugh at this fool ? " responded the chief. " He wants sandals to last him seven years, and behold in seven days he will be lifeless." * At one place they met a wizard who was foretelling times and things, giving counsel to many who sought him, at which the satanic monarch laughed again; and to Benajah's inquiry replied, " The blind fool ! he foretelleth things to others and doth not know that a rich treasure is buried right beneath him."

After many such incidents that astonished Benajah, they at last reached Jerusalem, and Ashmedai was introduced to King Solomon. The court rose to do homage to his satanic majesty, but the demon chief, heedless of this, grasped a cane and marked on it the measure of four garmids† and hurled it toward where Solomon sat enthroned. When asked what this meant, he said, " Behold a king of dust and earth, who, when he dieth, four garmidim will hold him; and yet he is not satisfied to hold all surrounding countries in subjection, but had yet to subdue me, the prince of spirits ! Why, O Solomon, didst thou thus de-

rejoice when they rejoice, but rejoice not when they weep, nor weep when they rejoice, for such is a demoniacal nature.

* This is intended to teach us the lesson that we should not covet, but feel contented with our lot, and not wish and desire for what we do not even know whether we will live to enjoy.

† A certain measure—about thirty-seven inches.

ride me?" "Pardon," said Solomon, "I have not derided thee, nor have I subdued thee for my own aggrandizement, but for the sake of seeking thy information as to the whereabouts of the Shamir, in order to enable me to build a sanctuary to the service of the Most High—mine and thy God." "I have no control over the Shamir," said Ashmedai. "It is under the protectorate of the prince of the seas and waters, who entrusted it into the care of the prince of the hills and mountains, held by solemn oath and obligation for the responsibility of that insect." "Where is this prince of hills and mountains to be found?" asked Solomon. "He is to be found," said Ashmedai, "in a barren wilderness, where the feet of a human being never trod. He is a *wood grouse*, flying to and fro, carrying with him the Shamir on all his journeys." This information gave Benajah another charge. He was directed now to seek the abode of the prince of hills and mountains, and he traversed through forests and deserts until he espied the barren rocky mountains described by Ashmedai. He searched carefully every place until he finally found the nest of the wood grouse filled with young ones. A happy thought came to his mind, and in another instant he had a stone rolled over the nest, and then withdrew to watch and wait for results. Fortunately it was not long before the bird-prince came flying along, and seeing a stone rolled over the nest of his young ones, he descended and tried to open the nest, but his efforts were in vain. Swiftly he flew away, and soon returned with the Shamir, placing it on the stone in order to cut it asunder; at the same instant Benajah struck a loud noise which frightened the wood grouse away, and Benajah leaped from his hiding place to the Shamir, grasped it and drew homeward. All attempts of the wood grouse to regain it were futile; and fearful of the account he had to give he forced his neck between two rocks and choked himself to death. The Shamir was brought to Jerusalem and the gorgeous temple was built.

Long had the house been completed and Ashmedai was yet held captive by Solomon for the sake of obtaining such knowledge from him as he could learn from none other; but the spirit-chief was so reticent that to all of Solomon's catechizings he would answer nothing beyond the explanation of his deportment while on the road with Benajah, his captor. One day Solomon became too inquisitive, and as they were alone in the royal chamber he asked the demon chief to show him some of his power. " Demand it not, O son of earth!" said Ashmedai, admonishingly, "for thou wilt surely rue it." "Rue it?" observèd Solomon amusedly. "Nay, I have never yet rued whatever I desired and whatever I demanded." "If this be so," said Ashmedai, " remove this chain from me, and give me thy ring for only one moment." Without consideration Solomon removed the chain and handed him his ring. The same instant the black demon arose to a monstrous size; his large, fierce black eyes were glowing like fire; his lips were opened in a grin, disclosing his ivory-white, needle-

pointed clenched teeth; and ere Solomon could
realize his terrible condition three thunder-like
crashes were heard, which burst asunder the
canopy and roof above them, and he was swung
out into the air with the ring whirring after him.
Solomon was thrown away to a distance of over
fifteen hundred miles, into a strange land, and the
ring flew above the sea where it fell, burying itself
in the bottomless brine. Ashmedai now assumed
the form of Solomon, seating himself on his throne
and reigning as King of Israel, with none to know
the imposture.

As Solomon awoke from his stupor he found
himself a stranger in a strange land, forlorn and
destitute;* then it was when he chronicled the
words, "What profit hath a man of all his labors
which he taketh under the sun?" (Eccl. i. ;.)
Three years he wandered in this position, often
repeating the words, "I, the preacher, was king
over Israel in Jerusalem" (Eccl. i. 12); but he was
laughed at. In the land of the Ammonites he succeeded in obtaining a position at the king's kitchen
to assist the chief cook, in which capacity he
often found opportunity to display his wisdom,
whereby he attracted the king's attention. The
keen eye of the princess, however, discovered in
Solomon a superiority, and she became infatuated
with him. Solomon, appreciating her generosity,
reciprocated the love, and regardless of her high

---

* This is intended for a lesson that when we live in affluence not
to be haughty and vain, but be mindful of how suddenly our position
may change; to be, therefore, ever meek and kind.

and his low position they were united in wedlock. This drew the displeasure of the king upon the couple, and he passed sentence of death on both ; but Solomon's eloquence aroused the paternal feelings of the king toward his own child, and he changed the sentence to that of banishment into a barren wilderness.

Again Solomon was destined to wander, but this time he had his faithful, loving wife, Naamah, to share his misfortune. Together they were ready to live or to perish. Jerusalem he feared to seek, for he thought that Ashmedai had his ring, the instrument to destroy him with, so he had to look for other quarters for retribution.

It then pleased the Lord to cease punishing Solomon any longer for his past haughty conduct, and brought him and his wife safely into a city. With a few pieces of silver he had yet in his pocket he proceeded to purchase some victuals, and seeing some fishermen he bought a fish which he handed to Naamah to prepare. She opened the fish, and, to her great surprise, found in it a heavy gold ring of peculiar make and of great value. On the ring was engraven a name she could not read, and amidst joy she called for her liege who at once recognized it as his ring.

With praise to God on his lips he placed it on his finger and his sorrow vanished.

It was the ring which Ashmedai flung away and fell into the sea ; a fish had swallowed it, and the fishermen caught the fish which the Lord had destined to be brought to Solomon, by virtue of which he and his beloved Naamah soon reached Jerusalem.

He sought the counsel of the wise men, but who could believe Solomon's declaration? Benajah was then summoned and asked his opinion; and he was the first that paid credence to Solomon's narrative. He gave his reasons that the king formerly loved him and consulted him, while the present king returned hatred for love, and that he was but seldom admitted into his presence.

It was then deemed advisable to usher Solomon into the king's presence and see the result. This was done; but no sooner had Ashmedai beheld Solomon with the glittering ring on his finger than he flew out through the window and vanished.

Solomon again ascended the throne, but such was his fear of demons that he had ever thereafter sixty valiant men to guard his bed when he slept at night (see Songs of Solomon, iii. 7–8).

Solomon now summoned the king of the Ammonites to appear before his presence; and after some preliminaries he made himself known to him. It is useless to say how glad he was to recognize and accept him as son-in-law, whereafter a great feast was made, and the king of the Ammonites returned home joyful and happy that his daughter was alive and in glory as the wife of the wise king Solomon, who now reigned over Israel in Jerusalem.   —*Gittai*, 68 *col*

GEMS FROM THE TALMUD.

The signet of God is truth.

Say little and do much.

First learn, then teach.

The ignorant cannot be truly pious.

Teach thy tongue to say *I do not know*.

Few are they who see their own faults.

Do not rely upon thy own understanding.

Rejoice not when thy enemy falleth.

Who aggrandizes his name,
He diminishes his fame.

Rather be the tail of lions than the head of foxes.

The measure one meteth with is meted unto him.

Light shines equally as well to a hundred as to one.

Who would need a light,
When the sun shines bright?

It is futile to open the eyes when the heart is blind.

Hospitality is as essential to religion as divine worship.

Happy is the pupil whose teacher approves his words.

Wisdom God giveth only to him who hath wisdom.

As the wine goes in the secret goes out.

May your fear of God be as the fear of man.

No vessel like peace can hold blessing.

He whose head is narrow has [generally] a broad tongue.

Go to sleep without supper, but rise without debt.

Silence is good to the wise, how much more to the fool?

Silence is the limit of wisdom.

Beautiful are the words of those who practise what they teach.

Respect the children of the poor, for from them proceeds the law.

Cast no mud into that well whence thou drawest water.

When two quarrel, the one who ceases first is the wiser.

Love peace and pursue it—love all thy fellow-creatures.

A miser is to be considered as wicked as an idolater.

Thy secret is thy slave; set it free and thou becomest its slave.

Love those who correct thee more than those who flatter thee.

The ultimate end of all laws is to unite in love all mankind.

He who will not listen to thy words, refrain from speaking to him.

Let the honor of thy pupil be as precious to thee as thine own.

The just of all denominations have a portion in the future reward.

Let the financial standing of thy associates please thee as thine own.

Where the teacher is disrespected the name of God is profaned.

Thy yesterday is thy past, thy to-day thy future, thy to-morrow is a secret.

Grasp for little and thou mayest secure it ; grasp for much and thou wilt get nothing.

If thou sittest amongst wise men be more inclined to listen than to speak.

Wrong neither thy brother in faith nor him who differs from thee in faith.

Man may become known by three things, viz., his purse, his cup, and his anger.

There are some who preach beautifully but practise not this beautiful doctrine.

Like birds of one feather flock together, so children of man to their like.

Do not utter a thing on mere assumption that it will come to pass.

To relieve thyself of doubt, appoint thee an instructor.

Judge not thy associate until thou hast been placed in his position.

In whatsoever the spirit of man findeth favor, the spirit of God surely findeth favor.

The indestructible monument of the truly pious is their good deeds.

Wisdom secluded within itself is like a myrtle in the desert—it rejoices none.

Not the commentary (of divine law) is the principal object, but the practice of it.

Refrain not from accepting the truth from whencesoever it emanates, even from inferiors.

He who cares not to hear one word (of reproof) may have to hear later many words.

Man sees a mote in his neighbor's eye, but a beam in his own he cannot perceive.

An instructor appoint thee, but an associate thou shalt purchase; and judge everybody deservedly.

Where the book (law and intelligence) is, there is no sword, and where the sword is, there's surely no book.

Where there is no law there are no manners; where there are no manners there is no law.

Where there is no wisdom there is no fear of God; where there is no fear of God there is no wisdom.

Where there is no knowledge there is no understanding; where there is no understanding there is no knowledge.

Where there is no flour (food) there can be no law (the study of it); where there is no law there is no flour.

The best preacher is the heart, the best teacher is time, the best book is the world, and the best friend is God.

Know whence thou comest, whither thou goest, and before whom thou wilt have to give account in judgment.

If I will not provide for me, who will? If I am to provide for me, who am I? And if I provide not now, when shall I?

Despise not any man, nor disregard any thing; for there is not a man who hath not his time, nor a thing that hath not its place.

If one induces another to perform a good deed, it is as meritorious in him as though he had performed it himself.

If a word spoken in time is worth one piece of money, silence in its time is certainly worth two.

The world *stands* on three things, viz., on law, on (divine) service, and on the practice of charity.

The world *exists* on three things, viz., on truth, justice, and peace.

Happy is the generation where the old listens to the young, but happier still is that generation where the young listens to the old.

Sins committed against God the day of atonement is given for their expiation, but sins committed against a fellow-man the day of atonement will not expiate, unless they are first pardoned by the injured fellow-man.

Have a soft reply to turn away anger, and let thy peace be abundant with thy brother, with thy friend, and with everybody, even with the Gentile in the street, that thou shalt be beloved above and esteemed below (in heaven and earth).

Do not attempt to appease thy neighbor at the moment he is in wrath, nor console while his dead lies before him. Ask naught of him at the moment he has made a vow, nor endeavor to see him in his adversity.

Man receives three names: One from his parents, one from the world, and one from his works. Which is the best one? Solomon has it: "A good name is better than good oil (the sweet perfume it bears)."

Rabbi Nechunia was once asked by his disciples: Wherewith prolongest thou life?" and he replied: "I never sought my honor at the expense of my associate's degradation, and a wrong done to me, its thought never went with me to bed."

Who is wise? He who learns from everybody. Who can be considered strong? He who conquers his own passion. Who can be considered rich? He who rejoices with his portion. Who is worthy to be honored? He who honoreth his fellow-creatures.

www.ingramcontent.com/pod-product-compliance
Lightning Source LLC
Chambersburg PA
CBHW020626030726
47497CB00007B/2434